# Magic Rewritten

## By Harlowe Frost

ISBN eBook: 978-1-959981-73-2
ISBN paperback: 978-1-959981-74-9

Editor: Weslee Imrisek
Developmental Editor: Elizabeth Daly
Developmental Editor: Dulaine Roode
Cover Art: Getcovers.com
Formatting: Huckleberry Rahr

*Books In the Magic Of The Galaxy Series*

## Series 1: Viera Kor

Book 1: Galaxy Lessons

Book 2: Magic Lessons

Book 3: Conflict Lessens

## Series 2: Betsy Doeth

Book 4: Conflict Reawakened

Book 5: Magic Rewritten

Book 6: Galaxy Revisited

*Acknowledgements*

This has been quite the year! Betsy's story is coming along nicely. It wouldn't be what it is without the assistance of my oldest son, who loves to brainstorm with me, you know you're amazing! Elizabeth Daly, your reading of my stories helps me flesh out every scene, and Dulaine Roode who will dig in and read my books for clarity and continuity better than anyone I know.

I want to thank Wes Imrisek, as always, for being the best editor. Your work in cleaning up my words thrown at the computer is mindbogglingly amazing. I am in awe of what you do.

Thank you, readers. You are why I tell stories. I appreciate your picking up the books I write and enjoying the escapism that I am thrilled to create.

# 1

## *A Child To Save*

### Betsy

Leaves lay over the parking lot and grass around the restaurant like a winter's blanket. A large branch from a tree had landed half in the bed of a pickup truck. Betsy surveyed the area, confused. None of the mess had been there a few minutes before. "You're saying I did this?"

"Yeah, that's what I'm saying." Violet reached over and squeezed her arm. "You just ... I dunno, were suddenly surrounded by a lot of wind. It was impressive."

Taking in a deep breath, Betsy nodded. "Okay, I'll think about that later. Right now we need to get to Oz. I don't know why Dulaine isn't in her house, but I do know that Pearl and her family are freaking out. We need to go and help."

The shock of Pearl's call and the frantic note in her voice telling Betsy her sister had disappeared from her bedroom still made her insides clench. The young lady lived in one of the most protected homes in a secure town ... there was just no way. There had to be a quick and easy explanation.

*I will find her and bring her home.* Betsy felt an urgency deep within her to save the girl.

Violet nodded and started typing on her wristband. Within a few seconds, the world around them melted and then reformed as the woods near the one-room schoolhouse the Katz family used for Dulaine's private tutoring.

"Is this the right place?" Violet gazed around. "We're in the middle of nowhere. Shouldn't we be in a town? Oz, right?"

"This is it. We're just not in the town proper. They don't have a landing spot yet. Come on, let's go to the family home." Betsy led them in a quick walk. It only took a few minutes to navigate from the school, through downtown, to the residential roads. The Katzes' home wasn't far from the center of everything.

As they sped down the path, Betsy called Ari, one of the other Pillars, and filled her in on the situation. She knew the older woman would email and update the other Pillars on what had happened. If they could figure anything out ... if there *was* anything to figure out, hopefully Dulaine could be found sooner.

In the back of Betsy's mind, she couldn't forget that she had a press conference in Dubai the next day, which meant she had to be there at six in the morning Wisconsin time. Soon, she may have had to call in one of the others to take over, as much as she didn't want to. There were several of them for exactly this reason, and she trusted all of the magically gifted wizards on Earth. She shook her head—at least the ones she'd known about her whole life.

At the door, they'd barely knocked when Pearl opened up, eyes red, sniffling. She looked down at her and Violet standing on the sidewalk. Her lower lip trembled. "Hi." She breathed in shakily. "Thanks for coming. Please come in. Help us."

They followed Pearl into the living room where her parents sat. Vicky stood. "Betsy, thank you for coming." Her face was tight. "We don't know what to do. We called the police, but they can't do much. They said they'd start a missing person report, put out an Amber alert, but beyond that there isn't much more they can do. There isn't any trail they can follow. She just disappeared."

She appeared keyed up, like a falcon soaring above its prey, ready to swoop in on any indication of where Dulaine may be. "Yes but let me search her room first."

Anger still boiled in Betsy. How could Dulaine, their youngest daughter, have disappeared from her room without a trace? There were ways, of course— she and Violet had just transported to Oz—but that would require alien technology ... and someone knowing about the child.

As they headed up a set of stairs, she thought about her phone. "Does Dulaine have a communication gem on her? Or maybe her necklace?"

Behind her and Violet, Porter's deep voice filled the small hall. "That's a good question. We did try, but we didn't get through to her. Our first instinct was yes. We all carry the gems with us and Dulaine loves that necklace, but it's late, and she was in bed. I'd tucked her in. She sometimes forgets and has those things with her ... she feels better with everything on."

Dulaine's bedroom had a tense stillness emanating from it. Betsy almost felt like she had to push through a veil to get in. The walls were painted a light green, and her furniture was lavender with highlights of dark blue. Her bed wasn't made. As Betsy slowly circled the space, she saw the necklace on the dresser.

"Here's the necklace."

Pearl hesitated at the door, then ran over. "Do you need it to find her? Are you ..." Her hand lifted a few inches. Her soft voice wavered as she asked, "Do you want it back?"

"No. It's attuned to your family. It likes you. Why don't you wear it?" Betsy slipped the chain over Pearl's head. A rigidity left the young woman as the pendant rested over her breastbone. Betsy felt Pearl's attention on her as she continued to search. When Betsy checked, Pearl's hand covered the magically imbued jewelry now attuning itself to her.

On Dulaine's desk, a jade stone was tucked behind the lamp under a piece of paper, as if it wanted to hide. *Why am I assuming motives for all these items? Not everything imbued has personality.* "Is this her communicator? Does she have others?" She pointed without touching anything more than necessary.

Pearl shook herself, then walked over. "Oh, yes, that's her stone. Where did you find it? I checked the desk already ... so did Mom."

*Maybe there's a sense of more than just magic in these items. I'll have to ask Elder Balzeno when he returns.*

"I don't know, but I'm good at finding things that want to stay lost. Not as good as some of the other Pillars. I may be able to get one of the others here tomorrow or Friday."

"That would be much appreciated, Pillar Doeth." Betsy noticed the formality right away as Vicky stood in the doorway. Her fear for her daughter upped this interaction to something official. "Should we wait to call the authorities, then?"

"No. Call them right away. They shouldn't be able to affect anything we can do."

The breath of relief from Vicky, and Porter, who stood behind her, was palpable.

Standing in the center of the room, Betsy's jaw clenched as she slowly spun in a circle, taking everything in. There was no sense of the girl. To Betsy, it felt like she had ... vanished.

"I'm sorry. I can't feel which direction she went. I will bring back someone with sensing magic. I hope that they'll be able to do more."

Pearl sniffled, but Vicky nodded, face tight. "I was afraid of that. Porter has called the authorities."

A boulder of frustration building in Betsy, she nodded. "I'll try to be back tomorrow. Either way, my friend who can do more than I can will be here. I don't know how or why Dulaine was taken, Mrs. Katz, but I want to find her and bring her home."

The side of Vicky's mouth twitched. "Me too, Betsy, me too."

# 2

## *Let's Give Them Something To Talk About*

### Betsy

The alarm cut through Betsy's dream like a knife. She groaned and rolled over, bumping into Violet, who lay next to her. Waking up with her relaxed some of the tension from Betsy's body and made her smile. "Morning, sexy."

"Hmm." Violet moaned. "Too early." She yawned and stretched, her lithe body rubbing along Betsy's seductively.

"As much as I want to pounce, we have just over an hour to be in Dubai, and on camera."

Violet buried her face in the pillow and groaned.

With a chuckle, Betsy kissed her shoulder, then pushed herself up. "I'm going to shower then dress. I'll meet you in the kitchen with food and coffee, lovely." As she gathered clothes, she gazed back at Violet's turquoise skin and violet hair and debated if she should do the dog and pony show au natural. *No, cooking naked isn't a great idea.*

Once clean, she headed down to her large kitchen and began making pancakes and sausage. Betsy knew she could use the panel to help with prep, but she liked to cook— it helped center her, and she didn't always have an excuse to do it.

The two ven flitted around, excited their staff were awake at last. Not that six in the morning should be considered 'at last.'

Wes, the black flying void of doom, landed on her shoulder, and she petted the overly-large-moth-like creature. He and Buttercup were still small enough to use her as a perch, but she wondered how long until they were just too big.

Buttercup dropped down onto one of the stools, for all the world looking ready to order a coffee and a muffin for her breakfast.

Violet walked in wearing a light blue knee-length dress covered with tiny flowers. It had a fitted bodice which accentuated her curves and a flowing skirt that flared out from her waist. She looked put together and professional ... and awake. It wasn't fair.

Her smile widened when she took in Betsy and the ven. "Ah, the villain and the princess, I see. So, what did Buttercup order?"

Betsy chuckled. "I was wondering the same thing. Though I don't have anything for her, I do have pancakes, sausage, and eggs for us, if you're hungry."

Face softening, Violet smiled. "Gods, I may love you."

"I'll believe that when you really are awake and well fed. Now come, sit." Despite her bravado, and all jokes aside, Violet's words struck Betsy harder and deeper than she'd expected.

As soon as Betsy and Violet transported to Dubai, they could hear the protestors outside the facility. The exact words weren't audible, but the chanting nature of the people was. Juk came up to Betsy, a wide smile on his face.

She clenched her jaw for a second, quickly composing herself into a neutral expression. "Juk. I didn't expect you."

His eyes twinkled. "I know, I know. I didn't intend to surprise you this morning, but I haven't had a chance to meet Xantay. I know she's planning on being here." He looked first to the left, then to the right, checking behind her, as if the SUV-sized dragon could hide there.

"The qynad isn't here, Juk." Betsy took a slow breath. "I wanted to check out where she'd be landing before I called her in. If there wasn't enough room for her, I didn't see reason for her to appear."

"Oh! Right." He blushed. "I get it. But you don't have to worry. I've already made all the arrangements. There's plenty of space for all three of you in front of the cameras."

For a second Betsy tightened her jaw, forcing her face to remain blank. "Okay, and will the audience be able to get through the protestors?"

He blanched. Betsy worried about how many emotions he threw off. She also wondered if he'd be willing to play poker and how much money he'd bring to the table. He wouldn't be the first DICKS agent she'd wiped the game table with.

Juk gazed over his shoulder at the wall most of the noise could be heard through. "Right, them. They seem to think the government is stealing people away." A chill ran down her back as she tucked this away to bring to the other Pillars. "This may be something all of you need to address today if there's time. As for the people asking questions, there's a path, don't worry."

"Okay, so where can Xantay transport in?"

Juk's spun. "Oh. Well." His cheeks puffed out as he blew out a breath.

Violet sighed. "Have the people started filling the room for the press conference?"

"Yes. It starts in ten minutes." Juk began to look and sound frantic.

"Okay, why don't you show us around?"

One of the local show runners came up. "You're needed on set." Then he shook his head. "Um. No ... ah ... English." He wasn't speaking English and a quick check showed me Juk wasn't wearing his translator.

Juk's brows were tightly furrowed. "Where is Mohammid? He was who I was working with before."

"Juk, where is your earpiece? I'm tired of asking you this."

"Oh, it's ... well, I just..." His stammering began to really frustrate her.

She turned to the runner and waved her hand, indicating he should lead the way. As they walked, they passed an empty room. Violet put out a hand. She handed the man an earpiece and pantomimed what she wanted. Once he had it in, she asked, "Can we use this room for a minute?"

His eyes widened and his jaw dropped. "You speak my language?"

"Can we?" Betsy insisted. It would take too long to explain.

"Yes, but we only have a minute." He nodded.

Violet tapped on her wrist communicator. A few seconds later, Xantay shimmered in. Betsy worried the man would faint.

Betsy placed a hand on his shoulder. "Please, show us to the room."

Gaping, he made a few squawking sounds as he turned and led them off.

Juk gulped. "Hi, Xantay." He craned his neck to look up at her. "I'm Juk. It's very nice to meet you."

Xantay bounced a couple of times before following. "I'm so excited to be here and doing this. I hope to represent my people and your world well. I've been excited to be a good liaison and representative for years, and I don't want to disappoint anyone, so, thank you, Mr. Juk. I appreciate being included in this very honorable endeavor."

While Betsy and Violet covered their mouths, trying not to laugh, Betsy wondered if the two men would go into apoplectic shock. As always, Xantay spewed out more words than any being should be able to in mere seconds.

"I want to thank you all for braving the protestors today." Terek Samad stood a bit taller, as if the actions of the people in the audience physically made him proud. "As you can see, as a reward, we have a new presenter besides Pillar Doeth and Major North. I was told we can just call her Xantay, which is her name. No title is needed. She is a qynad and comes to us from Grarrou as a liaison." He paused dramatically to let everyone take in the large red qynad with black markings sitting to Betsy's right. "If there are any questions, we can now open the floor to Pillar Doeth and her friends."

A wide, burly man in the center leapt to his feet. "Why do you surround yourself with aliens, Pillar Doeth? Why not bring other Earthlings to answer questions? And where are the people who have magic disappearing to? Is the government ... *your* government testing on them? Taking them out? Tell us the truth!"

As he stood there, shoulders heaving with his breath, Betsy worked to keep a neutral face. So much negativity spewed at her so quickly. "First of all, sir, I bring friends from other planets so that people will get used to seeing them. I could just come with humans, but I don't know if that would help bridge the gap between us learning about other beings and understanding who the aliens are. In my first press conference, the government was accused of not sharing information. By bringing different groups here, I ... *we* feel more people will learn who the different beings in our universe are." She sighed. "It is my hope that in the next few years more aliens will be able to come to Earth and seeing them will be a point of joy and pride for our people, not fear and hate."

The man's eyes narrowed, and he sneered, "That doesn't answer where you're taking the people who step forward admitting to having magic, Pillar Doeth."

"That's because we're not taking them anywhere. No one, as far as I know, has actually contacted the website."

"That's bullshit! My sister called the number on one of the fucking fliers in a coffee shop near her school." He was so mad, he was practically spitting.

Betsy lifted her hands but then let them drop. "Sir, we haven't put any fliers in coffee shops. Those are put out by colleges doing research. We *only* have the website. If people contact us there, we have a school set up in Africa. It's the same school us Pillars utilized to learn magic. Look, I'm sorry about your sister, and we can speak later about ways we may be able to help to find her, but understand, it wasn't us. We have no need to have people disappear. We know what we need to about what makes someone a wizard. We just want to make sure anyone with magic knows how to use it."

Xantay's head tilted. "If you don't want to speak with us about your missing sister, you can also contact the website, there's a form for that as well. Give us the information and we'll put her on the list of people we're looking for. She's not the only one who's gone to unofficial locations to find answers. The difference between those places and us is we've been utilizing this magic for centuries. We know how to help. And once people are in control of their magic, even while they're learning it, they can go home. We don't know what these other sources are doing."

There was a moment of stunned silence as everyone gaped at the dragon who spoke so eloquently. Betsy was amused and a bit stunned herself. She'd never heard Xantay speak so slowly. Finally, the man sat down. Though he didn't look happy, his anger had dissipated.

On the left side of the room, near the front, a girl stood. Apparently, this was going to be the pattern here. "Ms. Xantay, are you dangerous?"

The qynad's body quivered. "Oh, no, not at all. I'm as cuddly as a ..." Her speech halted.

Betsy leaned over to Xantay. "A teddy bear."

"Oh! Okay, yes, I'm as cuddly as a teddy bear, though, they kind of scare me."

The audience laughed and Betsy could feel the tension release.

A young woman stood. With a thick accent, she asked,. "Do qynads ... um ... well, are the stories correct? Do you hoard things? Like gold, or books?"

Xantay's tail twitched, then she shifted. "The word 'hoard' to us means something different than what you think. It is precious, but that's because it is our family. I believe it's similar to what you had in the past with your hippies—a group of several families raising their kids up together. Kids are encouraged to explore, then, when we are old enough, we apprentice or follow the adult that most aligns with our interests."

"Does that mean you ended up spending a lot of time *not* around your parents?"

"Yes and no." Xantay bobbed her head. "I loved doing what my dad did. I ended up following in his wing beats. That's what ended up bringing me here."

Another woman stood. "What about you, Major North? Do your people live in hoards or communes?"

Violet smiled. "No, we are similar to all of you. I grew up with my parents and siblings. But on my planet we're much closer to nature. If you were to see an image of the land, you wouldn't see the buildings."

"Are you criticizing how we live? Are you saying you're better than us?"

"No, just different." Betsy was impressed with how calm Violet remained. She wanted to slap many of the people in the room. "I rather enjoy the energy and way of life here. It's why I'm actively part of these conferences. It's also why I volunteered to be a liaison."

A man in the back stood. "I've seen my kids grow old, Pillar Doeth, and their kids. When I was a kid, I made the Earth move with my mind. I never told anyone. Does magic change a person? And why didn't it affect my kids?"

Betsy leaned back, giving the man all her attention. "Are the kids yours biologically, sir?"

"Oh, no. I adopted them. Why?"

"And how old are you?" Betsy wasn't sure she would ask, but this would get out eventually. Why not now?

The side of his mouth quirked up. "Well, I was born about a hundred and thirty years ago."

The crowd started to grumble, and a few of the smaller cameras turned to him. He looked to be in his twenties. Betsy smiled. "If you could stay after this ends, sir, I'd like to extend our talk. Like you, I'm a bit older than I look. I'm even a bit older than you. To give you a basic answer, yes, magic changes a person, and I'd like to invite you to be our first student at magic school."

3

*The Sense Of A Pillar*

Pearl

**P**earl looked at the clock.

Seven eleven.

She groaned. She'd barely slept all night because she'd been too worried about Dulaine. *Face it, there's no reason to stay in bed. May as well get up and eat.*

A pain throbbed in her neck and her body was stiff. Pushing up, Pearl collected the new shampoo and body soap Shanel had given her, Salubrious

Suds. She'd been promised energy. In the bathroom she collected the healing soap, Liveliness Lather. This was a morning for both.

Once she was clean, and feeling more awake and less sore, she dressed in jeans and a button-down and headed to the kitchen. The scent of coffee told her she wasn't the first up.

"Morning, Pearl. Bagel, cereal, or oatmeal?" Dad leaned against the sink, drinking from a mug. His eyes barely opened as she headed to the coffee maker, and from what she could see, they looked bloodshot.

"Did you get any sleep, Dad?"

"Not really. She's so young. I'm just so worried." He licked his lips, then jerked as the toaster popped.

He turned, got his bagel, then lumbered to the table.

Pearl decided to make some oatmeal. She made enough for Mom in case she wanted some when she came down. Once it was made, she sat at the table with a bowl. She added nuts and dried fruit and poured herself a second mug of coffee.

Mom came in, eyes wide, gazing around the room in jerky motions, as if taking note of everything and everyone. "Morning." She collected her breakfast items and joined them at the table.

Pearl sighed. "So, what's happening today?"

Mom took a bite of the hot cereal. "Word spread ... you know how it is. Even here. My email was flooded last night because of Dulaine and her disappearance. The town is worried. They knew that the press conferences were happening, but they thought we were insulated. Now with this ... we're having a town meeting tomorrow."

A knock at the door stopped any follow-up questions. Pearl's gaze jerked to the wall as if she could see who stood there. She noticed her parents were doing the same thing. "I'll get it." She pushed off the table, curiosity taking over.

"Who's knocking at eight in the morning?" Dad mumbled, sounding annoyed. "Don't they know we need to be at work soon? The store opens at eight-thirty." He got a far-off look on his face. "If we open up today."

Ignoring him, Pearl looked through the peephole and saw Betsy. A shiver of hope shot through her, and she threw open the door. "Betsy, did you figure anything out? Do you know where

Dulaine is?" She heard her parents clamor to pile up behind her.

"I'm sorry, no. I just came from a press conference in Dubai. I should still be there, but there were others who took over to finish up for me. I ... well, this is Zuza, he's another of the Pillars. One of his proficiencies is sensing. I thought he could try to follow any trails ... you know, see what he could determine."

Pearl realized there was a man standing behind Betsy. He was a bit taller than her with brown hair and the brightest blue eyes she'd ever seen. He looked older than Betsy. *My God, how old is he? If she's almost four hundred years old, is he like a thousand?*

She slowly shut her mouth when she realized she was gaping at him. "Sorry, hi. I'm ... um ... Pearl." She held out a hand.

"It's a pleasure to finally meet some of the people of the famous city of Oz." *My God! He has an English accent!* Pearl thought she could melt into a puddle then and there.

He shifted his gaze behind her. "I'm guessing you are Mr. and Mrs. Katz?"

Mom chuckled. "You can call us Vicky and Porter."

"Lovely. then you must call me Zuza." He bowed his head. "If I can see where your daughter disappeared, I'll start my search. Then, if it's okay, I'd like to look around town."

At her parents' nod, they head off with Zuza.

Betsy put her hand on Pearl's arm to stop her. "If it wouldn't be too much to ask, do you have any more of that coffee I can smell?"

"Oh, sure. Do you want some oatmeal, too? We were just having breakfast."

Betsy, who usually had a perfect poker face, looked pained. "Yes, if that's okay. I actually ate earlier, but it's been a grueling day and I'd love something more."

Pearl scoffed. "It isn't even eight. What all could you have done?"

"The press conference was at six, our time. It lasted an hour. I'm usually there for another hour. I probably would've been there for two—there was a wizard in the audience—but our government contact was there and one of the other Pillars transported in. I knew Dulaine was a priority and Zuza was available. I wasn't sure when you and your parents needed to leave for the shop, so," she waved her hands out to the side as if presenting herself, "here we are."

Sipping her coffee, Pearl wadded through everything Betsy had said. "Wait, another wizard? So, someone like you? How did you figure it out? Can you sense each other?"

"Maybe, if I'm close to them, but he asked why he'd lived so long. That's usually a pretty good give away."

Again, Pearl's jaw dropped. "Wait, he asked in front of everyone, on camera?"

Betsy chuckled. "Yep. It was a spicy press conference. Xantay was there as well. I'm not sure what will get more press. One of those two items or the protestors."

"Gah! I need more coffee." Pearl got up and filled her mug.

After a few more minutes, Zuza and her parents walked into the kitchen. "Betsy, you're right. The girl just vanished. If I didn't know better, I'd think she had been transported. But for that to happen, one of us would've been involved." He sighed. "I think we should check around town. I'd like a better feel for the area."

Betsy put her dishes in the sink. "This may take some time, and it won't be interesting. I wouldn't mind one person acting as a guide," she faced the family, "but if you need to open the store, we shouldn't need all three of you."

After some discussion, it was decided that Pearl would take them around. Dad wanted to, but she won the coin toss.

The three walked towards the small school where Dulaine spent her days. Zuza's head swung around as they walked. "Tell me Pearl, Betsy told me everyone in town manipulated the magic all around you."

"Yes," she said quickly. "Until we met Betsy ... um, Pillar Doeth, we didn't know there was more than one way to access magic. In the last three weeks we've learned so much. Our town thought we were safe, but after Du-Drop ..." She trailed off, her gut clenching with emotion.

Betsy rubbed her back. "I don't know how anyone could have learned about your town. No one spoke about Oz. Your people as well as mine know how to keep secrets."

"It's true. That's why this is so strange." Zuza stopped as they walked down Main street. "Betsy, there's another wizard in town nearby. You said the girl was a wizard?"

Pearl grasped his arm. "Where? Where do you feel her?"

His eyes closed. "No, I don't think it's her." His head swung around, then he pointed at a store. "Whoever it is ... they're in here."

Shock rocked through Pearl. *Is it Cassidy? Is my best friend a wizard?*

"One of the paper witches?" Betsy checked out the times on the door. "But the place isn't open yet."

Pearl grunted, then yanked on the door knowing at this late hour of the morning it would be open. "Cassidy, Trent, Jesse! It's me, Pearl. Who's here?"

Betsy and Zuza followed her in.

From the back, Cassidy squealed. "Oh, my God, Pearl, I didn't think I'd see you today." She ran up and engulfed her in a hug. "I'm so sorry about Dulaine." Her head shifted. "Oh, Betsy is here ... with a friend. Did they find her? Do they know what happened?"

They separated, and Pearl squeezed Cassidy's hands. "No, not yet. This is Zuza ... oh, um, Pillar—"

"Just call us Betsy and Zuza. Don't worry about formalities here," Betsy cut in.

"Right, Zuza is another one of the Pillars. He has the ability to sense things." She bit her lip and gazed up at him, uncertain what more to say.

A warm smile spread across his face. "Hi. I assume you're Cassidy?" He held out a hand.

Cassidy's eyes widened, and she shook his hand. "Yes. My dads are Trent and Jesse. They're in the back."

He nodded. "Would it be possible for us to meet them as well?"

She shook her head as if breaking away from a spell. "Yes, of course." She turned and yelled, "Dad! Pops! There's someone to meet you!"

Cassidy's parents came out from the back. Their gazes met Pearl's and softened. Trent came over and gave her a hug. "I'm sorry. Tell us how we can help."

Jesse followed suit next.

Then she introduced them to Zuza.

Betsy rubbed her face, the stress of the last few days feeling like a second skin tightening around her. "I don't know how I missed this when we first met. I was pretty distracted and you two were on the other side of the store … and sensing is probably my worst proficiency."

Zuza snorted. "Still no excuse. For the next few months you need to be better."

"I know." She sighed.

Both Trent and Jesse looked at the Pillars and then each other. Finally Trent narrowed his eyes. "What? What are you two talking about?"

"Like Betsy, I have magical specialties. Mine are gas, which means, amongst other things, I'm good with air and wind. My second is sensing. It's why I'm here. I don't know Dulaine, but I know she's a wizard. I'm trying to find her based on what I felt in her room as well as looking for any wizards in town. Right now, there are three wizards in this room."

A stillness came over Cassidy and her parents. Cassidy's eyes widened and her jaw slackened. Trent's eyes narrowed even more and Jesse, like Betsy, had a perfect poker face.

"In my opinion," Zuza continued, "having this extra magic," he closed his eyes for a few seconds, "imbuing, which isn't surprising —well, it *is* but not in this town—and gas, like me, the person should think about formal training."

"No," Trent said. "No one is leaving Oz. We've watched over our own, trained our abilities, figured things out for years. We can continue to do it. We learned ... what, witch magic? We can learn wizard magic as well."

Jesse shook his head. "I disagree." He sighed and turned to Trent. "Remember when I told you I was frustrated about Dulaine's disappearance and knocked all those papers onto the floor?"

Trent gasped. "What are you saying?"

"I'm saying, I didn't touch anything, love." He leaned over to kiss his husband, gently. "Emotion built in me, and then the air in the room just moved. It wasn't something I actively thought I could control. I wasn't sure what was happening."

"Was it the first time?" Betsy's focus narrowed to the third person in the room with her style of magic.

He shook his head. "I never knew what it was, and I'd never had so many emotions behind it before. I always just ignored it."

Betsy nodded. "Can you still create fire?"

There was a candle near the door. He walked over and focused on it. His body tensed, but then a flame erupted at the tip. "It ... yes. I felt like I had to fight through layers of internal commands. I could still find the path, but only because I've done it so many times before."

After a moment, Trent walked up and wrapped his arms around him. "Are you sure? Do you really think you need to go to this school?"

"Yeah ... I think so," he choked out. "I have this new beast of magic within me ... I'd like to really understand it."

Anger and resignation oozing from him, Trent turned to the Pillars. "Where is the school and how long will my husband be gone?"

"It's in Africa," Betsy said calmly. "The time depends on him, though with his basic understanding of magic, I don't think it'll take too long."

Cassidy stepped forward. "Can Dad go with? I can run the store. Or is this some private thing for wizards only?"

Betsy and Zuza gazed at each other, then they both shrugged. Betsy said, "It's fine by us. More than that, with our instant travel, Trent could still work here part-time and be in Africa part-time. The biggest issue is the time difference."

Trent's brow furrowed. "Instant travel?"

"Yep, it's how I was at a press conference in Dubai from six to seven this morning, and here now."

Once they got everything worked out at the store, they continued their search. Zuza placed a gentle touch on Pearl's arm. "Is there a high place I could oversee most of the town?"

"We have a water tower."

"Perfect. I'd like to blanket the area with my search." A shiver ran down his back. "All these years, we never thought about looking for more wizards. This process isn't easy, but it could've been done."

Once they got to the tower and climbed up, Zuza stood, searching the land in front of him. Pearl wanted to say she could feel the power emanating from him, but in reality she didn't.

After a few seconds, she realized watching him didn't make sense. She looked out over her town, and pride swelled in her. She loved Oz. Then worry seeped in. *Is Dulaine out there?*

Finally, she turned to Betsy who also shifted from looking at Zuza to the town below. Then she made eye contact with Pearl and smiled. "This won't take much longer. Zuza is one of the best."

"One of?"

"It's a long story, but yes."

"There are two more wizards in town," Zuza said, "over there and there."

Pearl followed where he pointed. "You pointed at the library and supermarket. That could be just about anyone."

"Well, we'd better be off. I'd suggest the supermarket first. If I need to, I can repeat this search again."

In the end, and after a lot of explanations, they found three wizards, but none of them were Dulaine. Jesse, Soleil, one of the librarians, and Aldo, a bagger at the grocery store, all agreed to transport to Africa for training on Sunday.

There wasn't anything more the Pillars could do.

"We're not done, Pearl," Betsy promised. "I'm going to continue my search. But we now need to look outside of Oz."

"*We're* not going to stop searching," Zuza corrected.

Despite her frustration and feelings of defeat, knowing these powerful people were on her side made her feel better.

*Stages Of Grief*

Betsy

Before heading back to London, Zuza returned to Wisconsin with Betsy for lunch ... or for him, dinner. They got barbeque ribs and cornbread muffins to go and brought them back to her place.

They sat outside eating and watching the ven fly around, enjoying the woods. Betsy leaned back in her seat, fingers sticky with sauce. "I don't know if we should consider that a success or a bust. Three wizards in that town."

Zuza chuckled. "The two single people didn't seem to mind. It was like they thought the trip would be a fun vacation. But Jesse," he shook his head, "he and his family aren't happy about the revelation."

"Do you think Kafi will be able to keep up with his research and shift to teaching? All of us are suddenly swamped with duties."

With a sigh, Zuza shrugged. "I really didn't want aliens and magic to come out at the same time. I wonder if we should've somehow released the idea of magic slowly over the years. That way only the aliens would've been new to everyone."

"Maybe." Betsy bobbed her head. "Having all these new things happening to us at the same time isn't helping." She sipped her soda. "I wonder if we can convince someone in Oz to come in as a teacher. The fact that Jesse could do both makes me think some of the wizards may be both. Who knows? And if we could learn how to imbue ... I don't know, tinctures? Lotions? Some of what that town does is pretty amazing."

"Even if we can't do what they do, having them on our side is such an advantage."

Betsy snorted, thinking of Viera and her introduction to magic. "Let's keep Flower Prancer away from them if he decides to ever return. If they learn unicorns are jerks, they may never forgive us."

Zuza laughed.

Kafi ran his hand through his hair and blew out a long breath. "Okay, so Sunday night I'll be getting three new students?"

"Are you going to be teaching Galactic Standard?" Ania gazed up, over her screen. "Or are we only focusing on the magic?"

Marco smiled, excitement written all over his face. "Oh! I love that idea. We should have Galactic Standard as an option. That way, if any of them want to travel to any of the space stations, they'll be ready ... you know, beyond the earpieces." He looked down as if taking some notes. "I could head to the school. All of my research has been online. I know Kafi has been traveling around Africa. I can easily be on site full time helping out."

"I could drop in a couple of times a week to teach," Zuza added. "We know that a couple of the students have sensing and gas as their specialties. Not that that matters, but I'm used to teaching anyway. It's been a few years, but I enjoyed teaching our younger Pillars."

"I'll speak with the liaisons, see if any of them can spend time at the school." Betsy added a note to her never-ending list of to-dos. "I'm sure Violet would be willing, and Xantay. She could help with the variation amongst the different technologies or the vast array of aliens. There are lots of types of lessons we could offer. I'm also going to see if anyone in Oz would be willing to give lessons on their style of magic. The students could choose to take the classes or not, depending on their interests." She rubbed the back of her neck, trying to think of anything else. "If Balzeno returns, maybe he could teach something as well. The dwarves know more about imbuing than anyone."

Ania nodded as she spoke. "We need to include something about the changes in our biology. What makes being a wizard versus a regular part of their species? Omar really let the cat out of the bag at your press conference. I mean, it would have come out eventually, but finding out we had another wizard on camera wasn't ideal."

"Did you ever figure out where he came from?" Having left the press conference so quickly, Betsy hadn't gotten much of the man's story.

Kafi tried not to laugh. "From what we can tell, we think he may be your uncle, Betsy."

"For fuck's sake, my grandpa? He said his dad was Gandalf?"

The laugh escaped the younger Pillar. "He didn't know his dad well. He was only around until he was about six, but his mum described him a few times. It really sounds like him."

Betsy's head fell into her hands. "Gods above. That man. Why didn't he tell anyone?"

"Omar said before he left he placed a hand on Omar's head, shook his head, and said, 'What a waste,' then walked out." Kafi shrugged.

Marco gazed off into the distance, head tilted. "Has any Pillar had a kid who wasn't born a wizard?"

Ania slowly nodded. "It's rare, but it can happen. Our magic is very dominant, but once in a while there is a child born without. That said, we usually wait more than six years. Gandalf was careless. But, on another topic ... sort of ... I'm starting to look around here for a location for another school. Australia has a lot of land, and I have the time. Right now we only have four students, but if we end up with more than thirty, we'll need another location."

Once she'd finished her summary of down under, Zuza and Betsy filled everyone in on the search for Dulaine.

"So, we need to up our hunt for where these researchers are hiding their labs. I really wish we had the Ziner here or a person with a better sensing ability. Viera's power was amazing." Zuza sighed.

"I'll send Viera a message. I know she just got to Abritos, but she may be interested in helping us. It may be worth asking her to return." And one more item onto her list. Betsy fought to not droop. "The last thing I wanted to mention is that at the press conference there were a bunch of protestors. You may have all heard about it, but in case you haven't, you all should know."

Marco's head bobbed. "It's all over the internet. People blaming the government for misinformation, for the disappearances, for the attack, for just about anything. I think the press conferences help, but I don't know how much more you can tell them, Betsy."

Zuza sighed. "People are going through the stages of grief. Denial, anger, bargaining, depression, and finally acceptance. We're at anger. I just hope it doesn't last too long."

## 5

## *Always a Trail*

### Betsy

After the meeting with the Pillars, Betsy checked over her notes. She had a lot of things to do, and her worry for Dulaine colored most of them. She sent a message to Viera then began jotting down requirements on a program that she wanted to create to search the dark web for the missing people.

As she made notes on what she wanted, her phone vibrated. *Hi. Want to have dinner together?*

Though Violet's words were mundane, a tiny thrill shot through Betsy. *Here or out?*

It didn't take Violet long to agree to join Betsy at her place. They both arrived in the kitchen at about the same time and embraced. Betsy felt the hug down to her soul, as if the touch of the smaller woman aligned something within her that had been slowly shifting out of place.

With a sigh, she stepped back. "Pizza? Pasta? Tacos with vegemite?" She laughed as the last was mentioned. On their last visit to Australia, Betsy had bought the horrid stuff so that Violet would have it when she ate over.

"Oh! I'd love that last one. With sushi?"

"Gah! You do know that isn't a thing, right?" Betsy shivered at the common special on every Torville station.

Violet's sea-blue eyes widened, and her eyebrows shot up. "Please?" She sounded so pitiful that a laugh burst out of Betsy.

"Gods above, woman. Fine." She grumbled as she headed into the kitchen. "I can make tacos, but you should order up the sushi from the panel ... but wait about ten minutes."

"Yes!" Violet's fist pumped into the air and then she danced around the room.

It was almost worth it to see her reaction ... almost. "Okay, while I work, tell me about your day."

Violet shrugged. "Mostly boring. I've been checking in with all the chanzii on planet. I need to prioritize the order in which people leave. Even though Earthlings know about us, we don't want each and every one of our people outed."

"That makes sense." Betsy handed Violet some vegetables to prepare.

"Some are quitting their jobs and relocating here to the empty houses. It's partially dependent on homes selling." She began chopping lettuce. "The goal is to spread out the shifts throughout the world to make it less obvious."

"Are you bringing a ship back here to pick people up?" Betsy went back to preparing the meat and tortillas.

"Yes. One should be here in a few weeks." She put the lettuce in a bowl and started on a tomato. "It's just all the prioritizing." She sighed. "I'd say most of the chanzii are fine as things are. A few like me actively want to stay. But then there is a group who want to leave. They don't care if it's to a space station or to live on a ship, they just want off this rock. I've been talking with Thorn about what to do with them. They're not trouble or anything, just not happy."

"With everything that's been going on, I guess I hadn't thought much about all that. You're juggling a lot of people." The meat was almost done, and the kitchen smelled amazing. Betsy moved it to a plate and pulled the warmed up tortillas from the oven. "How many people are helping with logistics?"

"Enough. We have a committee. And don't worry, we'll have a report with the basic outline to you, the other Pillars, and the government, by the end of next week. Then we're planning on submitting something once a month."

Betsy chuckled. "I wasn't too worried. Well, maybe about your sanity, but not about the reports."

All the components of the tacos came together and while, with a shiver of disgust, Betsy grabbed the Vegemite, Violet went to the panel to order a selection of sushi. Betsy compiled the tacos al pastor onto a platter. Not knowing what Violet would want, she put together a couple of vegetarian tacos as well.

Everything got moved to the table. Betsy ate what she believed made sense. Tacos with guacamole—she had some she'd picked up at the store earlier. She left the weird alien additions to the gorgeous woman with bizarre food beliefs.

Violet had both vegetarian and al pastor tacos on her plate. She spread a very thin layer of the condiment on the shell of the taco—the Vegemite, not the guacamole. She only dipped some chips she ordered in the yummy avocado dip. Then placed two unagi nigiri pieces within the shell. At last, she took a bite and moaned. "Gods, this is what I've been craving. I can't make the tacos right, nor can the panel. Your cooking is *so much better*."

Despite the compliment—and what that moan did to her—Betsy wasn't sure it was worth thinking about what the other woman put in her mouth.

As her cheeks heated, she re-evaluated her last statement.

Once the dishes were clean, Betsy pulled Violet in for another hug. "I need to check an update on the computer. It should only be about twenty, maybe thirty minutes ... then bed. Is that okay?"

"Of course. If you don't mind, I'd like to update Thorn on everything you told me at dinner. I know you told me you sent Viera a message about Dulaine and the other wizards in Oz," she couldn't hold back her own smile or soft laugh. Their conversation about the irony of the name had been fun. "But I'd like to fill in the Commander as well."

"Of course."

They separated. Betsy went up to her office, and Violet headed to the living room to log into her computer.

Once she'd turned on her system and the three monitors, it didn't take long to dive down into the dark web. She wanted to set up a few nets to see if she could catch anyone looking for magic or magic users.

The searches would take time; her programs had to be quiet. The code wasn't complicated, but if she wanted it to be effective, it couldn't be sloppy. Betsy wanted to spend a few extra minutes fine-tuning her work before launching it into the wild.

Her focus when she delved into the dark web always felt similar to being on a spaceship flying to a GPS transport. Everything around her stilled. Her every sense was on what she was doing. There was no other way to ensure no mistakes.

If everything worked the way she planned, the ball of thorns she created stuck into any other search that met her criteria. The beauty of her work was that it grew. As the minutes, hours, days, an—hopefully not—but potentially weeks went by, the net would eventually cover everything. No one would be able to look for black market magic without her knowledge.

That kind of insight, that kind of growth, that kind of power, took time.

As frustrated as she was that everything was so slow, Betsy felt better having set the program up. She was pretty sure no one could trace it back to her. The geniuses who taught her no longer played these games.

When she looked up, her eyes dry from practically becoming one with her keyboard and three monitors, Violet lay on the office couch, eyes shut. *Is she asleep?*

Her chair creaked, and Violet's eyes opened. "Oh, are you done? When you're focused on those monitors, you get lost."

"It's true. I need to get into a headspace where I'm totally working on the code so that I make sure it all performs how I want it to." Betsy stretched, all her muscles feeling tight.

Violet's eyebrows rose. "It looks like you need a backrub. Can I help you with that?"

"Hmm. That sounds amazing."

They headed to the bedroom and Betsy stripped down to a tanktop and panties. Violet ended up in even less, much to Betsy's excitement. Her luscious breasts a distraction for only a moment before she gave a command. "Okay, Betsy, on the bed. I was serious about the massage."

Betsy lay on her belly. "Oh, I wasn't in doubt or going to dispute it."

Warm hands began to knead her shoulders. The chanzii, as a race, were strong, and it didn't take long for Violet to work Betsy into a puddle of goo. Her neck, arms, and back muscles bowed down to the expert fingers on the woman perched above her.

Then Violet slid her hands up Betsy's back, under her shirt. She leaned down and traced her tongue up Betsy's neck, then kissed behind her ear. "Tell me to stop. That it's late and we both need to sleep."

"Hmm. But what if I don't wanna?"

With a slight tug, Violet worked Betsy's top off. Then she slowly kissed down her spine, ending at the top of her panties. Violet's warm hands skimmed down her sides, her fingers tickling her breasts as they lightly played down to the top of Betsy's panties, then hooked them, pulling them down her legs.

Violet nibbled at her ass, biting and licking, on her way down her legs, stripping Betsy naked.

Then her hands, magical in their ability to turn Betsy into nothing but heat and need, wandered smoothly down her body. Betsy panted softly, wanting nothing more than those hands and that mouth on more of her skin.

"Flip for me."

Betsy wasn't sure she could, but, wanting to participate, she forced one of her arms to obey, and got to her back.

She looked down and saw Violet's glowing eyes sparkling, as she began kissing her way back up Betsy's legs. The warm heat of Violet's mouth as she swirled her tongue and licked up Betsy's inner thigh made her core muscles clench with need.

Her back arched up and she moaned when Violet's fingers outlined feather-light designs on her other leg.

She was practically whimpering when Violet's tongue licked up her center, ending at her clit, flicking. Her breathing became rough and shallow.

"Play with your breasts, love." Violet's breath aroused Betsy's most sensitive skin, and she groaned, following her directions.

Her mouth dipped back down, sucking and stimulating her clit. Fingers began to pulse in and out, and Betsy's body trembled.

The pleasure grew with each wave. Time slowed and Betsy felt herself get closer and closer to breaking.

"Come for me, love."

Violet's mouth did ... something and Betsy squeezed her hands a bit tighter, intensifying everything, and her world fractured in an orgasm.

She wasn't sure what she screamed out as she bowed tight and arched high.

When her breathing calmed, Violet lay cuddled next to her, her head on Betsy's chest. Betsy wasn't sure she could think, much less move.

Violet yawned, then wrapped her arm around Betsy, giving her a tight squeeze.

"Tomorrow morning, I get to taste you."

"That sounds like a threat." Violet chuckled.

"Maybe it is," Betsy said, voice low and seductive. Right before she fell asleep she decided Violet would become a priority in her life. She'd spent too much time alone and the small time she'd spent with the distractingly alluring alien had begun to show her something she'd been missing.

6

*Change Of Plans*

Viera

Viera gazed at the field spotted with circular and oval platforms. Most were on the ground, but a few were raised a foot up. The smallest of the platforms was probably the size of a small living room ... *maybe medium. It's so hard to tell when the only thing to judge it by is the vastness of this outdoor space.*

She sighed and walked to the only rectangular area in the center of the visual beauty. It had two desks, one a beautiful bluish wood with stylized flowers sculpted on the sides and down the legs. There were seven drawers for her to store things in, and the top was so smooth, her hand tingled every time she rubbed the surface. She wasn't sure if it was the electronics or magic.

The other desk was modern, black, glass, and a metal she could only guess at. The center of the top was a console. The sides and the back angled down and were covered in small solar panels to power both the digital pad and data ports Viera's eventual students could use ... when she got students.

She couldn't get students until the classroom—*is this a classroom? Doesn't it need to have walls to be a room?*—was set up.

"What do we do if it rains?" Viera peered up at the clear sky, then down to Scout, who stopped chasing a creature that appeared to be a miniature flying ... *is that a purple bear? Flying?* It was only a few inches tall. "Scout, what are you chasing?"

"It's a r'vo-hat, Ms. Kor. They're really friendly. Well, they usually are."

"It looks like a bear."

He laughed. "I know, right. The ones on Earth are so big and scary. These guys are friendly."

"Are all the animals like that? Their twins on Abritos have different personalities?"

Staring up at the sky, Scout took a few steps to close the distance between them. "Some are different, and the r'vo-hat don't look like Earth bears. Not only are they smaller, their colors are different—well, except for the black ones."

Despite the beautiful day, there weren't many creatures in the field or the sky around them. *I wonder if that's why they chose this area for the school.*

All of a sudden, Scout's eyes widened. "No, I'm wrong, there's one animal that is exactly the same on both planets." He slapped his knee and laughed. "Avoid the r'su-ro at all costs!"

"Okay, I will!" She said, nodding in complete agreement. "It may help if I had any idea what a ... um, r'su'cho? Was?"

"R'su-ro," he said again, with some finality. "Trust me. They're mean." His eyes narrowed to a squint. "Oh! That's it. The cobra chickens! That's what they are."

"A goose? Your planet has geese?"

"Yes! And they're mean!" Scout spun on his heel and gazed at the different sections of the school. "Oh! I missed this kind of learning environment. I mean, I loved your class, but being inside all the time was so stuffy."

Viera had to remind herself that though Scout looked young, he'd been in classes for years. Age was so funny, and on this planet, they aged so much slower. She remembered her questions. "Right, but what do we do if it rains ... or snows?"

Sounds ... words, something Viera didn't understand, came from Scout's mouth.

She hadn't worn the earpiece because she knew it was just the two of them and she didn't need the translations, Scout spoke English. Now, standing in a field in the middle of an alien planet, it occurred to her how idiotic that had been. If they'd been separated and she ended up finding a chanzii who hadn't come from Earth .... She slapped her hand on her forehead.

Eyes wide, Scout gaped at her. "Are you okay Ms. Kor?"

"I'm fine. I just didn't bring my magical earpiece of understanding whatever it was you just said."

The ground shook, very slightly, and a clear dome appeared over them. Heart beating double,

Viera realized her mouth hung open. "What ....?" Nothing else would come out.

"It's a dome. We can ask the panel to collect it from storage when there's bad weather. That's what I just said. I can teach you the words if you want." He said it so matter-of-factly. Viera had to get her feet under her before classes started. As much as she knew how to teach in Wisconsin, she was beginning to wonder if she could handle Abritos.

Scout slid his hand into hers. "Ready to head home?"

"I am, though, I've been so busy today, we haven't had time to talk. How are you doing? There aren't many other kids."

"No, but I've been talking to Tiffany, and she said her parents may come as soon as a few weeks. I know that the planet isn't ready, but we're trying to work out Tiffany spending part of her time with us and the other in the ocean. The cambpulpo don't really need much. They spend most of their life looking like octopi. The rebuilding isn't important to them."

"That's amazing. Then you'll have a friend all the time, champ." Though Viera sounded upbeat, she really wondered what Thorn thought of the early self-invitation of the negative family. She loved Tiffany, but her parents were another story all together.

At dinner, a delicious stew full of vegetables and meats Viera decided she'd learn about ... later—there were so many other things to learn first—they discussed updates on the rebuilding efforts.

"I'm surprised how fast it's going." Viera leaned back, sipping tea. "I know having most of the population off world allows for quicker fixes, but I'm used to weeks or months of construction back home—you know, winter and construction, the two seasons—I forgot things could go faster."

Viera smiled wide. In the week or so she'd been on Abritos, Viera was still getting used to how different things were. It had been over a month since she'd left Earth, but a lot of that had been travel. The short timeline made everything feel like it'd just been a vacation ... a trip. Despite that, there were things she missed about home.

She loved Thorn and Scout and being on Abritos, but with everything being new ... she missed easy and familiar.

"... so we may be able to repopulate sooner than I thought. All of the majors organizing in the key planets are arranging chanzii in order of desire and priority. We may have everyone home in under two years." The giddy joy in Thorn's voice brought happiness to Viera.

There was a lull in conversation while they all ate. Then Thorn tapped the table with her finger. "Have you received any communication from Betsy or anyone else on Earth?"

Huffing out a small laugh, Viera shook her head. "You know, I've been sitting here all maudlin, missing the easy familiarity of Earth, yet I haven't checked for messages in two days. With the school and learning Galactic Standard ... I've been too tired to do much when I get home."

"Why don't you quickly check?" There was a strain in Thorn's voice that worried Viera. *Is there something wrong with someone in my family? Is someone sick or hurt? Did someone die?* She realized if anything like that were true, Thorn would've told her.

It didn't take long to pull up the note.

*Viera—*

*With the influx of information about magic and aliens, there have been some people who've decided to do their own research on magic. You know how people and researchers are.*

*With so few Pillars and government officials to gather new wizards (and witches ... I'll explain later) into our new schools, some of the new magic users are ending up in these research groups instead of with us. Some are disappearing.*

*Those people we met in the conference room after that big assembly, one of them has a younger sister named Dulaine. The other night she disappeared. Zuza used sense to help search their town ... she wasn't there. We're worried the groups that are doing their own research have stopped waiting for volunteers. They may have become more proactive.*

*Besides the loss of this eleven-year-old girl from a town of witches, the world is in chaos, but we're working to educate and inform.*

*I know you just arrived in your new life, but if there were any way you could find the time to help us locate this girl, all of us here on Earth would be grateful.*

*Real work is hard, my friend!*
*Betsy*

She read it twice before looking up at Thorn. "Did she write you as well?"

"No, Violet did. I just wasn't sure what you thought of it all." Thorn leaned back, concern filling her green eyes.

Viera sipped her tea, needing a moment to relax and let all her thoughts settle. "Part of me thinks I should go back and help. My sensing magic isn't trained as well as it could be, but it's better than Zuza's. If Betsy is worried about this girl and has any idea about where she could be, I may be her best bet."

"You're not wrong. And it isn't like you can't go back and return." She nodded. "Right now there aren't really any kids on the planet. You're spending most of your time learning the language, setting up the school, and hanging out with Scout. If you took the Ziner and Scout with you, I think it makes sense. While you're gone, I could make sure the final parts of the school are done so you can start teaching right away."

Counting on her fingers, Viera sorted her thoughts. "It's five days between here and the space station ... maybe four. So we'll say a nine-day round trip. Two between Torville Space Station Number Six and Earth. That's thirteen. Two weeks of travel ... gah! So long! I should probably limit my time there to maybe a week tops. I know that you're bringing the first wave soon, and the school *will* be needed. I'll make sure to study during my trip." She bit the inside of her cheek. "And I'm going to miss you, too."

Scout started to bounce. "Then we can pick up Tiffany and her parents on the way back. If I let them know, the timing will be perfect!"

7

*A Meeting From The Other Side*

Betsy

Waking up, Betsy's head pounded. She was tired, and though she knew she had to get to Oz for their town meeting, she curled around Violet for a bit more snuggling. She'd promised herself she'd give herself time with the other woman, and that was definitely the first thing on her shortlist this morning. *Well, maybe coffee first ... but then Violet.*

Violet hummed, then turned over. "Do I smell something delicious? Did you cook breakfast?"

Being up as late as they'd been the night before with her program, then bed play, Betsy had ignored everything but her warm bed. Not even the start of a migraine had slowed her down, not with the beauty in her bed. Waking up, she hadn't focused on anything outside of the four walls of her room.

Now that Violet had mentioned it, she realized she could smell food and hear sounds coming from the first floor. With the protections on her house, there were very few people who could be making such a ruckus. "Hmm. Not me. We should get down there before any of the riffraff mess up my space."

With a lot of reluctance, she pushed herself from the warm bed, grabbed an outfit, and headed to the bathroom to shower. "Raincheck on our morning play ... and we're not putting it off for long. I'm going to be fantasizing about your body until I have you naked under my spell."

Violet laughed as she headed off.

Once clean, and much more awake thanks to the Oz shower products, Betsy dressed, gave Violet a quick kiss, and headed down. Violet promised to only be a few minutes behind her.

It wasn't much of a surprise when Betsy found Marco and Kafi clattering around, making a mess of her kitchen. "Okay, what is going on?"

Marco held up his hands. "Don't look at me, Kafi said it was noon, he was hungry, and he was making food. He relented with the idea of breakfast since it was only seven in the morning for you."

Kafi scoffed. "You said you were hungry, too. You just wanted something lighter, thus the pão de queijo."

The thought of the small baked cheese balls made Betsy's stomach growl loud enough for Marco to smirk. She sat at one of the kitchen stools. "And what are you making?"

"Shakshuka and fried plantains. I wanted to make sure we all had something to warm our bellies and souls before heading to Oz."

She rubbed her head. "And did either of you make coffee?" She sniffed and didn't smell anything. "Never mind." She headed to the panel and ordered two cups. She wasn't going to make Violet wait once she made it down.

After she had a few sips, and some baked cheese, she began to feel human. "So, you two are joining me in Oz?"

Marco smiled, "We wanted to see this town, learn about their magic, and thought a town meeting would be a great place to experience it all."

"Hmm." She sipped her coffee, hoping her head would start to feel better. "And when did y'all decide to crash my pad?"

A plate filled with shakshuka, and plantains slid across the island into her field of view. The food looked amazing. "Are you really complaining?" Kafi's low voice laced with his African accent almost felt like a massage.

Before she could pick up her fork, she shut her eyes and rubbed her forehead. She tried to take a few breaths, thinking about centering herself. *Would it be worth taking a few minutes to work my magic on my head?*

Hands rested on the back of her neck and the top of her head. Then the feeling of cool water flowed through her, washing away the pain. She moaned with the cessation. "Gods, Marco, you've improved."

"I've been practicing." He slapped her shoulder. "And why didn't you just come right out and ask? Regardless of my skill, something as small as that?"

It felt like she was floating. "It didn't feel small to me, my friend."

He smiled wide at her words.

The scents of breakfast seemed to grow, and she dug into the food in front of her. The spices of the dish danced across her tongue and she enjoyed it, especially without the pain of the migraine.

Violet walked in as Marco laughed. "A headache is one of the first lessons, you know that. You probably could've done it yourself, even with your lack of skill." His eyes danced with amusement. "Morning, Violet. Didn't know you were here. No worries, plenty of food, and I assume that's why Betsy ordered up two mugs of coffee."

"She didn't order any for you two? You're making us food!" She sounded indignant.

"We already had some. We can't cook without our fortification!"

A few minutes later, they were all sitting at the table enjoying breakfast. Kafi leaned back, a twinkle in his eyes. "Are you coming to Oz with us, Violet? Coming to see how the town runs a full meeting with only low-level tech? That's the part that I'm most interested in." He narrowed his eyes. "Should we leave our phones here? Turn them off?"

"Yeah, I'm working on that. I want to figure out if we can somehow protect our tech from their mojo." Betsy smiled, excited to have the boys along for the adventure. The fact that the magic used by the people from Oz interfered with technology interested her. Wizard magic played nice with phones and computers, unlike that of the witches. If there was a way to allow both types of magic to use items with mechanical souls, it would be a great benefit to everyone.

Betsy smiled at her friends. "But for now, turn them off. No reason to destroy a good phone, unless you need an excuse to get a new one." Her smile turned mischievous.

Betsy sat between Pearl and Kafi. Marco sat on Pearl's other side. After introductions, the two hit it off right away. Though Marco was really in his eighties, the two looked of an age and even Betsy sometimes forgot the youngest Pillar wasn't just out of his teens.

Once everyone knew each other, they all turned to the main attraction.

"People of Oz," Vicky stood tall on a stage in the open-air meeting. She held a wand with black onyx affixed at the top, like a true witch. She spoke into the gem, and like a microphone, it projected her voice throughout the audience, even in the back where their group sat.

Kafi leaned over. "Is that a microphone? I thought you said electronics didn't work for them."

"No, there's an onyx at the end of her wand. I swear I told you all about the gems. Weren't you paying attention?"

"I didn't realize how well it'd work. That's fantastic. I wonder—"

"Hush," Betsy waved her hand. "Later."

She'd missed some of what the mayor had to say. " —are scared. Trust me, I'm scared too. The foundation of our town has been secret for years. Who we are, what we are, and what we can do has been something we've kept from everyone. Then, in one terrible, global event, everything changed. Not only did we, as well as just about everyone else, learn about aliens, the idea of magic being real was put on the table."

She paused as people in the crowd made sounds of frustration, agreement, and aggravation.

Betsy wondered how much the people around her actually knew about the different types of magic and that some of their fellow town members were going to be attending school to learn something new.

"Rumors in Oz spread faster than glitter after a bomb's gone off." She paused for the laughs, then her voice shifted, became tight. "Most of you have heard about Dulaine." All the amusement died away as the spectators leaned forward. Betsy wondered if anyone even breathed. "She disappeared from her room, and as of yet, we don't know what got her or where she went. We have the authorities as well as the Pillars helping us. Believe me when I tell you, if Dulaine is findable, she'll be found."

To her left, someone stood and spoke into his own onyx. "What can the Pillars do that we can't? Not to be bold, Mayor, but isn't magic magic?"

Very little changed about the woman standing, leading the discussion, but Betsy could feel a shift. Was her stature taller? Was there something in her expression? She wasn't sure, but she was convinced something was different. Maybe Vicky needed to protect herself from the emotions she felt over her daughter's disappearance, especially in front of her people while on stage. "That's a great question, Edy. Thank you for bringing it up." Vicky's focus grazed everyone. "Over the last few weeks I, my family, as well as a few others in town, have gotten to know Pillar Doeth, one of five Pillars currently on Earth." Kafi reached over to squeeze Betsy's knee at the mention of her name. "And though we all use magic, it took a few meetings and discussions to learn that the way we access our magic and what we can do is different."

This got more of the people talking. Vicky cleared her throat. "I'm going to ask Devlin to come up and explain it to you. We all know how good he is at teaching us new things and he and Pillar Doeth had discussed the magic systems extensively." She stepped to the side. "Devlin?"

Betsy turned her attention to the people of Oz. She didn't know most of them, and watching as they learned about magic, its uses, and that there was so much more than they knew, was interesting. Some seemed pleased with the information, others annoyed. A few were excited.

A girl stood. "Will we be invited to learn more about wizard magic?"

Devlin looked toward the back of the crowd where Betsy and the others sat. In a wave, the crowd turned to see where he focused on. Both Kafi and Marco shrugged and peered at her.

Narrowing her eyes at them, she mentally said, *I swear you'll pay for this later.*

They both smirked, letting her know they got her threat ... and didn't take it seriously.

With a sigh, she stood. She dug her own onyx from her pocket, held it up and smiled at Devlin. "As of now, the schools are new and we're working out exactly how we're going to teach so many burgeoning students ... assuming we get what we assume is coming. Ideally, we'd include your style of magic in with ours ... so, if we can figure that out, yes, we'd love to find a way to show all of you our system." As the crowd began to get loud she held out a hand and shook her head. "I do want to remind you, learning our magic won't translate to you being able to use it. What we have is something within you, not just knowledge of it."

Betsy sat, allowing Devlin to continue with his lesson. Afterwards, Vicky took over with some general announcements for the town. "Back to our heart. If any of you hear from Dulaine or have an idea what happened to her, please contact her family. As you can imagine, it is the top priority right now." She waited as the people murmured. "Though magic is known, the Pillars are keeping Oz out of the news. We aren't sure how anyone found out about Dulaine, but we'd like the rest of you to keep living as we've always lived, keeping our existence and way of life private. The pillars will be around for a bit if you have questions or leads, and again, thank you for your time."

There were questions and answers, and everyone stayed respectful. At the end, a group came over to speak with Betsy, Marco, Kafi, and Pearl. Betsy had met some of them, but most were new to her. The people she met had genuine interest in how the magic systems differed, though everyone seemed excited that Betsy had and used an onyx.

Once people started to break up and head home, Betsy tapped Kafi and Marco. "Ready?"

Kafi nodded. "I am. I'm even more ready for Monday's first day of teaching. I spoke with Devlin. He has some great ideas."

Marco smirked. "You two go." He slid his hand into Pearl's. "I'm going to hang out here for a bit. Make sure everyone is managing their emotions well. A missing family member is big, and I want to help."

Eyes misty, Pearl looked over at him and gave a small smile.

## Alakazam

### Betsy

The bed was cool Saturday morning without Violet in it. A sense of loss hit her that she wasn't prepared for. Though Betsy knew the other woman had work to do, the nights they could share were a pleasure she was beginning to treasure.

Rolling onto her back, she stretched. A ruffling sound was the only warning she had before Wes and Buttercup flew in and landed on the bed beside her, one per side. "Well, hello there, my beauties. Do you want to go outside?"

They made tiny sounds, then cuddled in like furry cats. She sighed with the comfort they brought. Not as good as Violet, but close.

"Ah, maybe not. Well, since my next appointment is on Monday," she reached down to give each of them a pet, "we have plenty of time to lounge around and do nothing."

She scratched Buttercup's head. "Did I just mess up my weekend of lounging around on my butt? Did I? I bet I did. I guess I'll be running wild with the two of you instead!"

Buttercup made a low purring-type sound and pushed into Betsy's side. Wes nosed at Betsy, reminding her he was there and willing to answer ... or rather, not answer her questions as well.

Her phone buzzed, and she realized she'd dozed off again.

Looking at her phone, she saw a text from Marco. It was time to face the world after all. First the demand of nature and a trip to the bathroom, clean clothes, and coffee from the panel in the kitchen, Betsy opened her phone and admitted the rest of the world existed and had to be interacted with.

*Betsy, we have a family in Colorado who say they have magic. Can you meet with them this afternoon? Their contact form has been emailed to you.*

The serenity of the kitchen seeped into her as she debated her response and the sad realization she'd have to leave her property. *Why is this coming from you? Are you monitoring the website?*

She finally stood and began making breakfast.

*No, it wasn't me. I got a frantic call from Juk. I'm not sure how he got my number, but apparently you weren't answering your phone.*

Betsy chuckled. *I only have three missed calls from him, and he didn't try texting. I was asleep. I've had a really busy couple of weeks.*

Marco's response didn't take long. *Oh, we saw Violet there yesterday morning. I know how busy you've been getting.*

She sent an eye roll emoji as a bagel popped. She added peanut butter to one side and jelly to the other then grabbed an orange.

*Okay, I'll arrange a meeting with this family. I'll also text the boy.*

Marco sent a thumbs up and Betsy put down her phone.

She sent a quick text off to Juk, telling him she'd contact the family in Colorado. Then she opened up the email. It didn't take long to arrange a meeting with them at their home at three in the afternoon, their time, just an hour earlier than hers ... not as bad as most of her globe-trotting.

She finished eating, cleaned up, and took the ven outside to play. She had time in her lazy morning and wasn't about to mess it up with duties.

*How long has it been since I was in Colorado? Have I ever been to Colorado Springs? No wait, I have ... I've visited Garden of The Gods, maybe twenty—fifty?—years ago? It's beautiful.*

Betsy blew out a big breath as she walked down the street gazing at the moderate sized homes. A lot of them looked similar. *What is this obsession with developers making every house look identical? Would it be that hard to give homes personalities?*

After double checking the address, Betsy walked up to the house and rang the doorbell. It took a few moments for a woman, a bit shorter than her, with long dark wavy hair, to answer the door. "Oh!" Her eyes widened, and Betsy saw how dark they were as well. "Pillar Doeth? It's you, from the TV? Like, you you?"

"Well, yes. It's me. Who were you expecting?" One of her eyebrows lifted with the question.

"I'm not sure. But you're famous, right? The person who travels the world and knows everything." The woman leaned left and right, gazing behind Betsy.

"Are you ... looking for something?"

"Are the others with you?"

Betsy wondered if she'd had enough coffee for this. "The others? Do you mean Major North or Xantay, or are you speaking about other Pillars?"

A blush colored her dark skin as her shoulders lifted towards her ears. "Oh, I meant one of the aliens. You're always with an alien. Are they all your friends?" Her voice was light and hopeful.

The image of Flower Prancer flitted through Betsy's mind, and it took work to keep her face blank. "Many of them, yes, but some are just acquaintances." She quirked a half smile. "Many of them I don't even know." A genuine smile spread across her face. "I assume you're Mrs. Reeve?"

"Oh! Yes. But you can call me Dulce."

Before Betsy could say anything back, a teen, a bit taller than Dulce, but otherwise very similar in looks, stepped up behind her. "Mom, invite her in."

"But, Trinity, it's *her*! Is our house clean enough? Is it worthy of a TV star?"

Clenching her jaw, Betsy refused to react to the idea she was any kind of 'star.' A lifetime of living in the shadows, and now she was known by anyone willing to turn on their television.

The young woman, Trinity, closed her eyes, though Betsy could tell she rolled them by the shake of her head. "She doesn't care, Mom, just let her in."

Betsy leaned forward. "Your daughter is right, Dulce, I don't care about the state of the house, just your ability to do magic. Trust me, I've seen worse."

Dulce bit her lip. "Okay, follow me. Would you like something to eat or drink?"

The words, "No, thank you." were on her lips, when the scent of something sweetly divine hit her.

"Um, sure, if it's no problem. I don't want to intrude."

Trinity scoffed. "You'd have been more of a bother had you said no." Then she skipped ahead.

Betsy was led through a spacious living room with warm beige overstuffed furniture. The tables were mahogany. Pops of oranges and navy brightened the area. The space looked professionally decorated. "Your home is lovely."

Dulce blushed again. "Thanks. Trinity wants to become an interior decorator one day. She watches the shows all the time."

The large room led into a dining room. To the side there was a huge kitchen with anything anyone would need to cook a feast. It wasn't as big as hers, but it was close. Trinity and a tall man, at least six feet, moved around the room, filling plates with cinnamon rolls.

He looked up and asked with a low timbered voice, "Would you like tea or coffee?"

Transfixed by the large gooey baked delight, it took Betsy a moment to realize that, though he had the same dark hair as the other two, his eyes were a light blue. "Coffee, please."

She sat at the table with the rest of the family. Mr. Reeve placed the plate down. "Pillar Doeth, I presume from my wife's startled exclamation a few minutes ago. I'm Jerome. Welcome to our home."

They shook. "Please, call me Betsy. I only see the need for formality in formal situations, which this is not." She took a bite of the roll. The sweet and spicy flavor exploded in her mouth and she moaned. "This is amazing."

"Thank you." Betsy started to wonder how many times Dulce would blush.

The four ate the treat in silence. Even the coffee was delicious ... and Betsy didn't like anyone's homemade coffee.

She leaned back. "Okay, so you sent a message to the website saying someone in the house had magic."

Jerome's face flattened. "We did, and I'm who you were emailing with earlier, but I'm not sure if any of this was the right decision."

"I understand, but not training what you have can be dangerous." Over the years Betsy had drilled her ability to sense to a low level. She couldn't do what Zuza did and she'd never be able to do what Viera was capable of, but small general information was at her disposal. She closed her eyes and sent out a small pulse of intent. She thought, maybe hoped, it would pick up Trinity. To her surprise, she discovered all three of the Reeves were wizards.

She finished her coffee and put her mug down, a small smile on her face. "Okay, from what I can tell, all three of you have magic within you."

The neutral to annoyed look that Jerome had been giving her turned downright sour. Despite understanding his annoyance at having this dropped on him, Betsy knew how important it was for all of them to take her seriously. Dulce gazed back and forth between her and her husband, as if trying to figure out how she should feel. Trinity smirked, as if none of this came as a surprise.

"What does this mean?" Jerome sounded angry.

"Ideally, it means you'd come to school in Africa," Betsy knew she sounded harsh, and worked to modulate her tone. "We have a facility already set up. I ... We'd really like it if you'd allow us to teach you everything we can so that you'll know how to use your magic."

"So," he spoke slowly, ticking items off on his fingers, "you want us to move away from our home, quit our jobs, have Trinity leave her school, buy tickets to Africa, and just remove ourselves from our lives?" By the end, his low tone had risen to almost a yell.

Betsy sighed. "When you contacted us, did you just assume it would be your daughter? Did you expect to have just her life interrupted?"

"I didn't contact you, she did. I just made sure I was here for this part. We've obviously lived this long with whatever is in us, *Pillar Doeth*. I respect your opinion that we need training, but I believe we've survived just fine without it."

His daughter bristled. "No, I disagree. You're choosing ignorance out of fear. Please, let's hear her out."

His face tightened, but he gave a nod. "Fine, tell us how our life will be completely uprooted and changed. I am right about that, aren't I?"

"Yes and no." Betsy tried to stay calm, despite his ire. "We can get you back and forth between here and there easily enough. It would be ideal for you to be in Africa full-time, but if that isn't possible, we *can* work with you. My hope is that you can take a couple of weeks' vacation, but if you can't, I'll speak with Kafi, the Pillar running the school. It's possible to do some of the lessons remotely and then have you come one or two days a week to make sure you're really understanding the intricacies of magic."

A mocking laugh boomed from Jerome as he crossed his arms. "And you're just going to pay to have my family fly back and forth between here and Africa once or twice a week? No worries? Us and every other family with magical potential?"

Betsy sighed, realizing this was getting her nowhere, fast. She lifted her wrist controller and tapped a few buttons. As the room disintegrated around her, she hoped the ven were outside. She wasn't sure she could explain large flying moths as well as transporting to the family she was bringing home with her.

There was a limit to what the family could handle in one day.

9

*A Room Without Windows*

Dulaine

Sleep weighed heavily on Dulaine. Her head felt stuffy and she wondered if she was sick. "Mom! Dad! Pearl! Can someone bring me water? My mouth feels pasty."

She wasn't sure how long she'd been in bed, but she figured it had been too long. *Where is everyone? Usually someone will help me if I'm sick ... am I sick?*

Dulaine squeezed her eyes tighter and tried to think about the last thing she could remember. She had been in bed. *So maybe sick.* Reading a book. *Hmmm.* No, magic. *I was planning what to talk to Xantay about the next time I saw her. That red dragon, grrr, qynad is amazing, and I want her to be my friend.*

Her mind began to make connections as it cleared. *Why hasn't Pearl or Mom or even Dad woken me up? Or brought me water? Or checked on me? Am I late for school? Kirke is going to be so mad at me.*

Every muscle in her body felt heavy and her eyes didn't want to open. *Is it morning? Is everyone else in the house asleep? Am I wrong about the time of day? I feel so tired.*

She forced her muscles to bunch under her, and got a hand braced, able to push herself up. With a groan, she forced herself to a sitting position. It took a conscious effort to convince her eyes to open.

Everything was dark.

*It must be the middle of night. I can't even see the outline of ... anything. Where is the moon or starlight?* Her head swung to her window and she squinted. Nothing.

Fear washed through her and she began to tremble. "Where am I?"

A surge of energy followed her fear, and she shot to her feet. Dulaine's heart beat hard and fast in her chest, and she began to breathe rapidly.

*Where am I? Where am I?*

She shuffled forward, her hands out.

A loud thump made her jump before her head caught up with her. *You just kicked something that shouldn't be there. Think, don't just react.*

Reaching down, she felt the object. If felt like a box. With caution, she moved around it. She waved her hands as she slowly made her way across the room.

*Wall, if I find a wall, maybe I can locate a light and figure out where I am. There has to be a window ... or a door ... or something to give me a clue to my location.*

It took a few minutes, but Dulaine finally made it to the wall. After that, it took ... time, she had no idea how much time of searching one way and then the other to find ... nothing. There were no switches that felt like any kind of light switch that she recognized.

When she found the bed going in one direction, she switched direction and went the other way. Returning to the cot, she flopped on the bed on her side. "Why didn't I feel for a wall first, before stubbing my toe?"

As she let the adrenaline seep out of herself, she focused instead on her family. *How long have I been here? Does anyone know I'm missing? Are they searching for me? Will they ask Betsy and Xantay to help? When will I see my Pearl or my parents again?*

A tear slid down her cheek as she thought about how much she wished she could return home to her own room.

A click echoed from high above and a sound like a hissing snake filled the area around her.

Her body began to feel heavy again as her eyes drooped shut.

*Why would anyone want to take me?*

10

## Going Viral

### Betsy

The silence in the house as Betsy landed on the coffee table in the living room only lasted a second, replaced by a pair of thuds and squawks. The sound had Betsy thinking about the ven but remembered they were playing outside today.

*Good thing my furniture is sturdy enough to handle my sudden weight.*

Dulce landed on a couch, but Jerome and Trinity ended up not having anything but air under their butts, and they both toppled to the floor. Betsy clenched her jaw to stop herself from laughing, then shot to her feet. "Okay, then, welcome to my home. This is probably the first and last time you'll ever be here, but it was the easiest way to answer your questions about how you could travel to Africa and home on a tight budget."

Jerome leaned on his hands and gazed up at her, slack jawed. Dulce sat sprawled on the couch where she landed. Only Trinity seemed to have any life still in her. "Holy hell, did we just ... *'Beam me up Scotty!'*?"

After thinking about it for a moment, Betsy scrunched up her face and wobbled her hand back and forth in a 'sort-of' motion. "Transporting technology is a bit like what you're asking about, but not quite. Though, yeah, we did just move in space from your kitchen to my living room."

Jerome narrowed his eyes. "Are you telling us that we're in Africa? We just," he waved his hand back and forth, "and now we're halfway around the world?"

"No. I'm not saying that. I'm saying we're in Wisconsin. I didn't want to go to Africa without warning the people there. If you *want* to visit the school, decide after meeting Kafi, we can do that. I just needed to stop you before your head exploded."

He pushed up and moved to sit next to his wife. "How much does it cost?"

The question didn't make sense. "How much does *what* cost?"

"Any of it? All of it? Transporting around the world. Attending the prestigious school. Becoming a wizard." His face was becoming a snarly mess again.

*I wonder if I could transport him into the pool. Would that cool him down?*

"This will all make more sense once you start taking classes—"

"If we take classes," he interrupted.

"Right." Betsy took a deep breath, reminding herself that zapping them was wrong. "But once you learn a bit more you'll understand why none of it costs anything. We don't need, nor do we particularly want, your money. We just want to make sure you're safe in using the magic within you."

Trinity leaned forward. She'd stayed on the floor sitting cross-legged. "Then what's the catch?"

"None? I mean, if, once you've learned everything we have to teach, you decide to help us with intergalactic relations, or world wizard teaching ... that needs a better name, then I'd—we'd—be thrilled. But that isn't a condition, it's just a dream. There are five Pillars. If we can build up our numbers that would be amazing. If we can't ... we can't."

Jerome leaned back and crossed his legs. "Does the job come with a retirement package? How well does it pay? What are the details?"

The laugh, somewhere between genuine and ironic, erupted from Betsy. There was no way to stop it. She shook her head as the family watched. Once she got her composure, she rubbed her face. "Again, these are questions for later. But, for now, would you like me to send you home, or would you like to visit Africa?"

"As you can see, we have a large plot of land. This will be the location for outdoor lessons." Kafi's arm swung to encompass the area. "We have dorms over there and the school building across this field. It has been several years since it's been in regular use, so we're all excited to have classes starting up."

Betsy's phone vibrated and she saw it was a message from Violet. She waved it so Kafi could see, then walked away. She heard Jerome ask, with some indignation as she made her escape, "Some years? You look to be in your twenties, and Betsy can't be older than me. You make it sound like it's been out of use for years and years. I don't understand."

Betsy looked over her shoulder and saw a tight smile on Kafi's face as he started to answer. Then she turned a corner and was out of range to hear any more of what they spoke about. As nice as the family was, she was more than happy to pawn them off on the other Pillar.

The text asked how Betsy was doing. She debated replying, but somehow her finger just ... slipped, and the next thing she knew, she called Violet.

"Hi! How are you?" Violet sounded happy.

"I'm good. I'm in Africa with our first family of self-identified wizards."

There was a small gasp over the line. "Like, they contacted the website?"

"Yep. Then Juk freaked out because I wasn't immediately available to respond."

"You weren't? What were you doing?" Her voice took on a low, sly tone.

Betsy chuckled. "Well, since I was out late last night with Kafi after the Oz meeting, and I could finally sleep in, I did. He emailed early."

Violet's laugh filled Betsy with joy. "I can just imagine him freaking out when you didn't email him right away. Then he probably debated if you knew what email was ... or a phone ... or technology. He probably sent out a smoke signal."

It took a few seconds before Betsy could respond. "Probably. Then he had Marco contact me. At that point, I'd finally woken up. Marco did the wacky method of texting me."

"Whoa! I'd have never thought to do that."

"I know. Never. Speaking of, why *did* you text me?"

"Oh! Yeah." It sounded like Violet was moving around her house. "I was going to invite you to dinner tonight. But if you're in Africa—"

"Oh, I'm not here long term. I'd love to have dinner." Giddiness bubbled in her at the thought of an evening with the beautiful Violet.

"Great! I'd offer to cook, but I want it to be enjoyable. So, Italian?"

"Perfect."

"One more thing." A seriousness laced her voice.

"Yeah?" Betsy stopped on her return walk to Kafi and the Reeves.

"Have you been online at all today? Xantay is everywhere. It's like they finally took note that she was at the press conference and suddenly everyone is all about the talking qynad. There are sound bites, images, memes, everything. It's mostly positive and she's probably over the moon, but you may want to check in on her or have one of the others do so."

Betsy sighed. "Right. I'll put it on my list."

As she walked up to the family, they all seemed less stressed. Dulce and Trinity even looked happy if that was possible.

When Trinity saw Betsy walk up, her face lit with mischief. "So, old lady, Kafi tells us you were brought up in a hovel with a dirt floor?" Both her eyebrows lifted in challenge.

"Oh, is that what he told you?" Betsy crossed her arms. Behind them, she saw Kafi smirk, though he was in a quiet conversation with Jerome.

Dulce's blush was back and her eyes grew to saucers. "No! No, no, no. He said nothing of that kind. He just mentioned that having magic made the wizards age slower ... long lived. He mentioned you were older than you looked."

"*Much* older," Trinity said, with feeling.

Betsy bobbed her head back and forth. "Well, Trinity, you're not all wrong. I eventually moved to a full cave ... it was amazing, it had a roof and was protected from the elements. But you know, then I was abducted by aliens."

"What!" Her eyes nearly bugged out.

One of Betsy's eyebrows rose.

Kafi turned from his conversation and sighed dramatically. "Abducted, Betsy, really?" Obviously, he'd been listening. "Is that the story you want to spread?"

A smile spread on her face and she shrugged. "Probably not, but I did spend the better part of a year on a space station."

He and Jerome walked over. "By choice, if I remember the story." She noted that Jerome seemed calm and much more at peace.

"Zuza and I needed to learn Galactic Standard. You've had better access to learn it and don't need to spend that time away, which is good since we never had the Pillars living here to cover for you to live that long in space. Though, in the next few years, potentially, everything here is going to change."

Betsy had a couple of hours before she was going to meet Violet downtown for dinner. She'd left the Reeve family with Kafi to figure out the logistics of how they'd move forward with their schooling. From what she'd overheard, they were set on getting lessons.

She was thrilled with the decision. The more students they had, she hoped the easier it would be for the transition for future potentials. Their goal was freedom of information. Getting the general population to believe they had good intentions wasn't as easy as she'd hoped.

In her home office, she quickly checked the dark web to see if her program had found anything.

Nothing.

Then she started surfing all the social media sites. Her feeds were filled with images of Xantay. A snort escaped her.

*I don't know what a qynad is, but dragons talk?*

*Did anyone notice the last press conference looked like an old fashion Japanese movie? The speech and the vocals didn't match, but I don't care, that dragon spoke to me!*

*Does she breathe fire? Is there a shoulder-sized one?*

*Can I be part of her hoard?*

*Beware! The dragons are coming to burn our world down!* The image on this one was from the krottel battle with two qynads in the sky breathing fire.

The memes kept going.

*Are there more now than when Thorn initially came out as the first alien on Earth?*

She tapped the small panel next to her. A moment later, Xantay's voice filled the room. "Pillar Doeth, how can I help you?"

"I was wondering if you were enjoying your new-found fame?" There was no way the tech master hadn't seen all the memes.

"Oh!" Her voice got lighter. "They're fun, right? I've been watching them grow. More and more of them. I've debated adding some. What do you think?"

Amusement filled her. "I think there are plenty and more will come all on their own. I don't think you need to worry about adding to the pool."

"Okay, because I have some amazing ideas."

"I'm sure you do, but let's give the humans their due."

Xantay sighed. "Okay. When do you think you'll need me next? Any sign of my new best friend?"

A boulder formed in Betsy's stomach. "We've been doing searches for Dulaine, but so far we haven't found her. You know you'd be top of the list if the girl was found."

"Okay, but let me know if there's anything I can do to help with the search."

Betsy debated having Xantay work on some of the tech searches. The problem was, she wasn't sure that was the best use of either of their time. "Any digital tracking you can perform to search would be wonderful. I'm working on one and the authorities are as well. You're better than anyone I know."

"On it. Anything else?" Her desire to help flowed over the line.

"I'll speak with you soon or have one of the other Pillars contact you. We'll likely have you help at the school."

A grumbling sound that Betsy translated as pleasure came over the line. "I'd like that."

# *If You Build It Here, They Won't Come*

## Betsy

Monday morning, Betsy woke up with Violet curled up next to her. She decided she liked having the other woman sharing her space. After years of living alone, she was surprised to discover part of her may have been lonely.

A sense of peace filled her as she pulled Violet in for a quick hug, then she kissed the top of her head.

Violet rolled, her dark hair spilling over the pillow like a fan. Her eyes slowly opened, then she smiled. "Morning, beautiful. I could get used to waking up to such a view."

Dipping down, Betsy caught Violet's mouth, slowly exploring its depths, loving her taste. She leaned down, spending time, not wanting to rush.

Eyes closed, enjoying the sensations, Betsy raked her fingers through Violet's hair, rubbing her thumb over her forehead.

A hand slid up under her tank, fingers gliding feather light up her side. Betsy moaned in Violet's mouth as she reached her breast, her thumb circling and flicking her nipple.

Betsy lowered down, straddling Violet's leg. She rocked, creating friction for both of them in a slow rhythm. Breaking their kiss, she trailed smaller nibbles down to Violet's ear, then traced the shell with her tongue.

Below her, Violet gyrated, rotating her body to match Betsy's pace. Violet spread her legs, increasing the contact as Betsy sped up her seduction. She sucked in Violet's earlobe, then gently slid it out of her mouth, scraping her teeth over the sensitive skin.

Violet's hands, which were now both under Betsy's small sleep shirt, shifted from light teasing of her breasts, barely touching, to more intense pressure, ending with special attention to the tip. Every time she teased, Betsy felt her body tighten and get closer to climax.

Her breathing was getting choppy as she traced her bites down Violet's neck.

Then one of Violet's hands slid down, under her panties, and began to play with her clit. "Come for me, beautiful. I want to hear you scream."

She was so close she barely knew what she was doing as she moved against the amazing woman below her.

Violet's hand shifted, slipping over her ass, and dipping between her legs. She found spots Betsy never knew were sensitive as her fingers probed and stimulated her.

Just as she began to tense, her world exploding in the creation of a million galaxies, Violet pinched her nipple, caught her mouth in a deep kiss, and slid a finger in her.

Betsy broke, the orgasm coming over her fast. For a few moments she didn't know anything but the pleasure of the woman below her, within her, kissing her, and then all her muscles turned to goo.

She tried to roll, but Violet held her tight. "Not yet. I like the weight of you on top of me. Let me enjoy this."

"Hmm," Betsy finally managed to say. After what felt like an eternity of heaven, she sighed happily. "Do I get to have my breakfast now?"

"No. I think we need to get ready for our meeting in New York. We're not allowed to be late, are we?"

Growling, Betsy slipped from the bed and stretched, then shifted her gaze between the dresser and closet. They did have a meeting with Juk this morning and all she wanted to do was spend the day in bed with Violet. She was very tempted to wear jeans. The dufus probably didn't even notice what she wore. *But the other people in the office did ... like Miranda. Damn, I should bring her something. She's been going above and beyond these last few weeks.*

With a sigh, she headed for her closet and rummaged until she found a pair of high waisted, straight legged, forest green slacks, and a sleeveless light blue knit top with oversized matching blue buttons on the left shoulder. She took the clothes, along with undergarments, into the bathroom and placed them on the counter. Then she stepped into the shower.

Once clean, she dressed and headed to the kitchen to start breakfast. Violet was up and, while she yawned, informed her she'd be right down.

The two had coffee and hot cereal with nuts and raisins for breakfast.

"What time do we need to be in New York? Nine?"

"Yep, it's always ten their time." Betsy finished off her food and sipped her coffee. "We should change that to afternoon and give us the morning to ourselves." She gave the other woman a wicked smile, then sighed. "Do you have any big projects this week?"

"From what I understand, the Ziner should be back in orbit by next weekend. I need to get the next set of chanzii selected, packed, and ready to go."

"By the weekend?" The idea floored Betsy. "That seems ... fast." *Hadn't the first group just left?*

"Oh, no." Violet shook her head, amusement radiating off her. "I think the crew will want to spend some time here, maybe upwards of a week.

They like the planet and will want time off the ship. I mean, it's only a week off from travel, but any excuse to come say 'hi.'"

"I get it. Will Thorn and Viera be coming?" Betsy would have loved to see her friend, but she couldn't imagine Viera leaving Abritos so soon after moving there. She had hoped for communication, but it wasn't fast or easy to send messages from that distance. Not if you didn't work for the government directly.

"I don't think so. Thorn's missive was short. It was sent several days before the Ziner left planet, though she told me that she's needed there. I can't imagine her coming here so soon after Abritos opened up." She stood, grabbed Betsy's dishes, and headed to the sink. "I could ask if you want."

"No. The Ziner will probably be here by the time her answer comes. I'll just wait and see if Viera made it. She may have decided after Thorn contacted you. Communication can travel really slowly."

"That's true."

Betsy got a towel from a drawer and wiped the table down. Once the kitchen was tidy, they headed to the panel and Violet dialed up New York.

The alcove area of the New York lobby, where the Pillars and other aliens were asked to transport, wavered into view, replacing Betsy's kitchen.

She looked at her watch. They had twenty minutes. "There's a coffee shop next door. Let's go get coffee and some pastries. I meant to bring something for Miranda. It won't be the best thing, but at least we won't arrive empty handed."

"I love that idea, and not because I want more coffee." Violet slid her hand into Betsy's and pulled her towards the door.

In the coffee shop, Betsy ordered four coffees, tea, and hot chocolate. The woman behind the counter smiled as one of the other baristas began on the order. "Would you like anything else?"

"Three breakfast sandwiches, sausage and egg each, and a variety box of your best pastries."

"Sounds good, I'll give you a selection of what sells best, ma'am." She started to tap on the screen. "That'll be—"

"Does the shop take business tabs?"

"Why, yes, we do."

Betsy smiled. "Put this on tab Frida-67311."

The woman behind the counter's eyes widened and Betsy sighed. "It belongs to Orson Mard, you can call to double check, but he'll verify me. You could also check with Miranda Tips for my clearance to use it."

The woman's face shifted from shock and worry to relief as she continued to type. "No, ma'am, knowing it means you have permission. All done. Have a wonderful day."

As they made their way to the elevator, Violet shook her head. "Why didn't you just pay?"

"The last two times I went out to dinner with Orson, he stuck me with the bill. It's become a game between us."

"Ah. So, should we get more before we head home?"

"Maybe." Betsy smiled. "It's more fun when he's with us."

Betsy held the drinks and Violet carried the pastries as they headed up the elevator.

When they got to the correct floor, they approached Miranda's desk. Violet practically vibrated with her excitement. It brought Betsy joy to see her happiness. Violet blurted out, "We have treats ... what do you want?"

Miranda's eyes narrowed and she started typing on her computer, then a smile spread on her face.

"You do know that account 67311 has been set to throw a flag every time it's used, right?"

"Yes, I count on it. I'd have used a different one if I wanted to be quiet about it. What's the fun of tweaking Mr. Mard if he doesn't know about it?"

"So," the secretary leaned back, a twinkle in her eyes, "what did the boss man buy me?"

Violet opened the box. "What do you want?"

After looking over everything, Miranda selected a bear claw. "You didn't happen to get anything other than coffee, did you? I love coffee, but I'm already vibrating in my seat."

"As it goes, my friend, I brought hot chocolate and herbal tea." Betsy winked. "I remembered how you always have a cut-off time for coffee."

Chuckling, Miranda grabbed both drinks and plopped them on her desk. "Well, this should keep me for a few hours."

In the conference room, Betsy looked through the box and selected a chocolate croissant. She was on her second bite when Juk made it into the room. "Hi, hi! I'm not late, am I?" He checked his wrist, but he wasn't wearing a watch.

Taking a long, calming breath, Betsy looked at her phone. "No, you're fine. We just arrived a few minutes early to bring Miranda a treat."

"Miranda?" Juk's brow furrowed. He looked around and when he didn't see anyone else, he sat.

*If you kill him, you'd have to start over with someone new, who will probably be worse.* "Mrs. Tips, Juk. Miranda is her first name."

His brows popped up. "Oh. I didn't know that."

A silence descended on the room for a few moments while Betsy and Violet munched on their treats. Finally, Juk took one, licked his lips, and tasted it. Then he said, "So, I have a few items on my agenda."

"Sounds good. Where do you want to start?" Betsy watched him closely, keeping a neutral expression. In the end, she wanted this to work. She eventually got all the others trained. She could work with this new pup, too.

"Well, I've been researching the items you brought to my attention. We don't have any of these religious fanatics in the US. I'm not sure if there's anything we can do about the ones in Africa or Australia, but I've assigned a team to keep tabs on them. The idea that magic is being used to harm is against everything I've been taught."

"Good. I agree." Betsy finished her croissant and debated something else.

"I do too," Violet added. "When you get these fanatics, it's important to make sure they don't grow unchecked."

"Next are the groups claiming to help the new magic users. Pillar Brzezinski is following the university in London, but we've found stirrings of something in Spain, Mexico, Tennessee, and California. There are probably more."

"Tennessee? Really?" Betsy realized she had to get back to her program and see if it had picked up anything in its net.

"Yeah, why?" Juk sounded confused.

"Nothing. It just wasn't the location I expected ... but is it ever?" *I'll need to adjust my program. I really should bring it to Xantay to play with.*

He huffed out a laugh. "No, it isn't." He leaned over and pulled the box of pastries closer to himself. Biting his lower lip he searched until he decided on a cheese Danish. "Oh! My favorite." Then he smiled with a low moan and took a bite. "Anyway, besides the religious fanatics and people who wanted to do research on wizards, the only other things I wanted to discuss were Oz, the missing child, their magic, and magic school."

"I assume you have people searching for Dulaine?"

Juk nodded. "We do. There is a case with a couple of agents who are working around the clock. We know finding her is top priority for you so it's top priority for us."

It was a shock to hear something come from him that she actually approved of. "Ok, what about magic school?"

"Well, you met that family. How many people are signed up now?"

Exasperation filled Betsy. "Not as many as I'd like. Maybe a half-dozen. But I'm hoping more will contact the website."

"After that family got back home, the daughter started to hit up social media hard with everything she'd learned. Apparently she has a lot of followers. Our site has been getting more hits. We don't know who all are actual wizards, but I've been sending the emails out to the different Pillars."

"Ania, Pillar Stewart, is finding a spot for a second school. If we do end up with a number of students beyond what we can handle in Africa, we'll figure out something there."

Juk's jaw dropped. "Why not here? America is perfect for this, no?"

"No." Betsy held back a laugh. "Look, we can do a lot in the US, but we don't have the reputation here. We're already leading the press conferences. We need to show that this is a global effort. Right now, you have me popping up all over the place to hold the press conferences. That means the others have to do the other parts, like running the schools. Kafi ... Pillar Owusu, whose family has been running the school for years, and Pillar Stewart in Australia are the perfect choices to lead."

His face hardened. "I just really think, especially if we're helping finance, that the school should be closer to home."

Violet cleared her throat. "I think I can help. I'll re-allocate some of the money from the sales of the homes to the education of new magic users on Earth. It is only a fitting thank you for the hospitality. That way, if you're really worried, you don't have to re-budget for this program." She pulled out her phone and tapped it for a few seconds. "I also believe there is a spot near the place the chanzii settled in Australia that would be perfect for a training facility. We could easily hand over the homes for dorms for students to live. All that would be needed are the buildings."

Despite the color of Juk's face indicating his wanting to explode, Betsy loved the idea. "We should contact Ania and let her know. I'm sure she'll appreciate any help you're willing to give."

"Oh, I should head down there and work with her for a few days."

The excitement in Violet's eyes didn't stop the disappointment Betsy felt in knowing she wouldn't be seeing the other woman much for the foreseeable future.

# 12

## *There's An App For That*

### Viera

Horax stopped Viera and Scout as they were about to debark on Torville Station Number Six. "Okay, this isn't a long stay. Juniper and I are doing a quick look over the ship, restocking, and then we want to get on our way to make it to Earth as quickly as we can. Viera, I know you want to get there to help."

She nodded. "I really do, and I appreciate all of this."

"Why don't you go to the promenade, get some food, then return. We'll be ready to leave in about two to three hours."

"Sounds great, Horax. Should we get anything for you?" Scout bounced up and down on his toes, then slid his hand into Viera's.

"No, but thanks." He turned and lumbered off.

With Scout dragging her, the two of them made it to the large open center of the space station in record time. The area was teeming with aliens, both on the floor and in the sky. The upper corridors emptied out a family of phoenixes, then ven. Before Viera could see more, a huge dark purple qynad trudged past them. It was the size of a truck ... or two.

Her heart pounded in her chest. As far along as she'd come in 'aliens are amazing' she still found them new, fantastic, and a bit terrifying.

Once the purple qynad's tail had passed, Scout continued to pull. "Let's go to Bob's place. He usually serves fancy food, but it's early so his place shouldn't be too busy, and I haven't seen him in a long time."

Viera found it hard to think and run at the same time. "Bob?" She was pretty sure she'd been to 'Bob's place' before. "Wait, is he the fing?"

"Well, not *the* fing, but he is one of them. He's a great cook and I think that's where we should go." Viera wanted to roll her eyes, but feared she'd fall over.

*What do I care about where we go? I can't read any of the menu items or store names. I'm still completely at the mercy of the kid.*

Scout ran up to the tall proprietor of the establishment and despite knowing the Bigfoot-looking alien was not only friendly, but was an amazing chef, her heart kicked it up to high gear for a few seconds as she took him in.

"Bob! Do you have a table for us? We're only here for an hour or two and we are hungry."

Dark brown hair covered Bob from head to foot. He wore what looked like a house dress a stay-at-home wife would've worn in the sixties. The outfit was covered in a pattern of psychedelic leaves and birds.

"Commander Firoza's son. I think I can put you and your friend in the corner. The human ... Viera Kor, right?"

"Yes." She was shocked he remembered her. She'd only been here one other time when she came with Thorn during spring break.

The side of his mouth quirked up. "Well, come along young Scout ... Pillar? Please join me."

He led them to a table deep in his restaurant. He handed them each a menu, but Viera still couldn't read Galactic Standard well enough to order. "Maybe we should focus my learning of the language with food and menus. I seem to be in this situation often enough."

Scout laughed. "How about the special from his planet? It's really good. It's like a meat pie ... spicy but sweet. I don't know how to explain, but I think you'll like it."

Viera shrugged. "Why not? If nothing else, I can eat on the Ziner later. It isn't like I'll go hungry."

It didn't take long for Scout to speak with their server and order the special and hot tea. He said it was similar to Earth black tea.

"So," Viera sipped the sweet drink, "Bob's outfit. Are the trees and birds native to his planet, or is the outfit ... just loud?"

Scout scrunched up his nose, but before he could answer, a low timbre behind her said, "It's his planet. It's a fun place to visit." Turning, Viera saw Balzeno walking up behind her. "Do you mind if I join the two of you?"

"Of course not." Viera smiled at the dwarf.

"Balzeno!" Scout called out. "What are you doing here?"

"My guess, my boy, is the same as you. I'm waiting for a ship heading in the direction of Earth. I had to leave and check in on my planet, but now I'm returning to become an ambassador."

As Viera contemplated his words, she realized her face scrunched and her head tilted. "You don't have your own ship?"

"No, youngling. I could, but it seems like a waste with how little time I spend in space. I can just as easily get a ride with the myriad ships flitting about."

The server came out and placed their meals on the table, then asked Balzeno what he wanted. They spoke for a few seconds. Viera just watched and listened, knowing the earpiece translated his words, but wishing the basic Galactic Standard was something she knew.

Balzeno's bushy brows came together. "Why do you look so glum, Pillar Kor?"

She shook her head. "Nothing." His face tightened. "No, really. I mean it. I just feel a bit like a child when I can't order for myself because I don't know Galactic Standard, yet. I'm slowly learning, I just worry it'll take years."

His face lit up like a light. "Is that it? Well we can fix that. Years ago I ... er, we dwarves invented a way to imbue a language into the mind of a being. As it goes, Galactic Standard is one of the easier ones. The process only takes a few days. If we head back to the ship, we can speak with the Commander. If it's okayed, I can get it started right away. It'll be done by the time we get to Earth, or close to it."

Viera bit her lip. "I don't want to be in a stasis when we arrive. Would I be in a stasis? I mean, I want to be ready to help when we get to Earth. There's a lost child ... I want to help find her." She quickly filled Balzeno in.

"Hmm. I'm not surprised scientists are trying to get between the new wizards and the Pillars. They're working with the government, and your world doesn't trust the government. A girl was kidnapped you say? Well, I'll make sure you're awake by the time we get there. If the language isn't complete, I'll give instructions on the completion for your return to Abritos. I can even add the Chanziian language. You should have enough time for both."

Excitement and hope surged through her. "Can I give you a hug?"

He laughed low. "Of course." The hug was huge, like hugging a bear.

Once they finished their meal, every bit as good as Scout promised, and gossip, they returned to the Ziner. Horax was fine with including Balzeno on the trip. He was an Elder, and one rarely said no to an Elder. As for the language training, he said that was Viera's choice.

They headed to her room, and she lay down on her bed.

"Okay, youngling, just relax. I'm going to have to use a specific gas to ensure you're asleep for the entire time."

"Gas?"

"A compound that my people created to ensure you're asleep the whole time and receptive to the lessons. It's safe.

"Um." Indecision slammed into her, but she really wanted to know these languages. "Okay."

Viera got comfortable and on his way out, Balzeno shut off the lights and locked the door. Then, just as her body began to relax, a hissing sound of gas being released filled the room.

# 13

## *The Growth Is Almost Magical*

### Betsy

A soft breeze played across the lake as Betsy and Violet walked the path, eating their ice cream, and avoiding the other people enjoying the day. The bike path hugged one of the two main lakes in Madison, and there were bikers, walkers, in-line skaters, people with pets, others with kids, and many more. The morning was beautiful, and everyone seemed to want to enjoy it.

"How goes the lottery of who gets to head back home?" Betsy asked before licking the sides of her cone before the drips got out of hand.

Violet watched her tongue dart in and out, doing its clean up job. "Good. There were a few that really wanted to go last month, and with the Ziner's return, they'll get to go sooner than planned." She took a bite of her cookies and cream. "I'm arranging to clear out the Australian town and have them move here. We have a lot of empty houses."

"Is there a rush?" Betsy didn't think the need for a second magic school location was that urgent.

"No." Violet confirmed her suspicions. "But I'm asking the chanzii who aren't ready to head off planet to relocate. Most of the ones I spoke with are willing to move here since there are plenty of homes. I want it to be a smooth transition. If they can't get jobs, I won't push them, however, if I can get some of them here and start to empty some of the homes, I think it'll be easier for Ania."

"That makes a lot of sense." They walked in silence for a few minutes, enjoying their sweet treat. "What are your other big responsibilities?"

The other woman laughed. "There are several families that want to move. A few towns, now that aliens are out, are actively anti-alien, anti-magic, anti... well, they're just anti. The chanzii living near those aggressively negative locations are petitioning, as a group, to leave. I have to work with both local authorities, the DICKS," she giggled after saying the acronym, "and the established chanzii neighborhoods to see what we can do."

"Are you thinking about placing them into the wild?"

Her head bobbed left and right. "It's a thought." She licked her ice cream. "Some areas are more welcoming and if we have a full subdivision, we may go that route." As they passed a trash can, she tossed her napkin. "Okay, tomorrow is a press conference. Where are we heading off to?"

It warmed Betsy that Violet had completely committed to join her on these adventures. She found she adored spending time with the other woman. "I'm heading to Africa this afternoon to see how Kafi is doing. Do you have time to come along?"

"I'd love to. My next meeting is in," she checked her watch. "just over two hours. If we head there now, I'm sure I'll have plenty of time."

They returned to Violet's car and drove to her house. After washing the ice cream off their hands, and texting Kafi, Violet dialed Africa, and they were off.

It was just after three in the afternoon when they got there, and they met out in the field. "Betsy! Violet! Welcome to Magic School!" Kafi gave each of them a hug.

Violet smiled wide. "How many students do you have?"

"We have thirteen, so a lucky number, but several others have contacted the website. It seems magic is popping up all over the place."

Relief caused a cascade of Betsy's muscles to loosen. She hadn't even realized she'd been so tense that people would ignore the website, the school, and their offer of education. "That's good, like really good."

"It is. Marco and Zuza are heading up the welcoming committee. We decided we'd only call on you if someone contacted us from the U.S. or we had too many people to speak with at once."

"Thank you." Betsy looked over at the buildings, now aglow with soft lights. "Are families choosing to stay here?"

"Some. Trinity and her mom are staying here, but Jerome is traveling back and forth."

"I take it you gave him a transportation watch?"

Kafi nodded. "I did. I had Xantay program it so it only goes from his family rooms here to his living room in Colorado. Until there are more safe landing spots, I didn't want to train him for world travel."

Violet tapped her phone. "There are a few more people who have contacted the website. I don't know if Marco has read these, but there is a group who say they *think* they have magic in Germany."

"Think?" Betsy pulled out her phone.

"Yeah. They said that a fire started in their house and they weren't sure how." Violet waggled her eyebrows. "Oh, and it happened in the center of town, as well."

Betsy rubbed her eyes. "Couldn't that just be ... you know, misbehaving kids? There has been fire longer than people randomly erupting with fire magic."

The three walked over to a class in session. Each of the students had a digital pad. Kafi smiled. "They're learning about where the power comes from. This is something I want to give to Viera when next I see her. I know Flower Prancer trained her with a lot of practicals, but I don't know if he's offered her any theory."

Betsy considered the comment. "I know the Ziner is coming back to gather more chanzii. Maybe we can send a care package to her. I can only imagine her being very grateful for anything we send."

Violet nodded wildly. "Definitely. I can make sure Horax, or whomever is commanding the ship, brings the package home to her."

Dulce put her pad down on the desk, placed her hand on top of the device, then shut her eyes. After a moment she started waving her hands above her desk as if she were tapping out a code. Then she stood and walked over to Kafi. "I believe my elemental magic is solid. Is there a way I can test?"

Kafi gazed at Betsy and lifted one of his brows.

Betsy laughed. "Fine. Yes, Dulce, come with me. Let's go play."

Her eyes widened, and, as was her habit, she blushed. "You? But Kafi is our teacher."

"True, but I'm the only Pillar with a proficiency in solid. My specialties are solid and life. So, I should be able to help you with this." Dulce bit her lip, then nodded. "Okay, let's head outside. I want to walk you through a few exercises. Do you know your secondary proficiency?"

"Secondary?" As they walked out, Dulce's shoulders rose and her eyes widened.

With a sigh, the two made it out to a bench in the courtyard. "Dulce, I'm just a person, like you, like Trinity, like Kafi. You need to breathe."

"Right ... breathe."

"Let's start with the dirt in that potted plant. Can you tell if there are rocks in the soil?"

"Rocks?"

"Yes, stones, pebbles? Anything in the dirt that isn't ... you know, dirt?" Betsy needed this woman to relax, and she didn't think yelling 'relax' was the way to do it.

"Oh. Um, let me think." She squeezed her eyes shut and her mouth slowly tightened into a small, compressed spot on her face. Then, as if the answer to a question she'd been contemplating for hours came to her, her face relaxed, ending in a creased brow. "Six stones, nine pebbles, and ... um, I think there's a dozen bugs."

Betsy snorted. "Ah, so your secondary proficiency is sensing. Excellent."

Dulce's eyes flew open. "It is?"

"Well, if you look at the wall of the school, can you tell me how many people are in the classroom we left by using your magic?"

"By looking through the wall?" Dulce's jaw dropped. Her reaction amused Betsy. It had been a while since she'd been able to teach, and she forgot how much she enjoyed it.

"Sensing through the wall. You'd be using both of your magics." Betsy put a hand on her arm. "If you can do this, we'll have to find you food. It'll take most of your energy. You'll build up more of a reserve, but for now, this will tap you out."

Finally, Dulce looked relaxed and started to smile. Her gaze raked over the building, and she focused for a few seconds. Her eyes narrowed then she nodded. "I see twelve people in the building. It's like ... I sense the heat ... so, I don't know. The alien, Violet, she's different than the others. But, then again, so is Kafi. I think it's because he's older. Violet may be different because she doesn't have magic. This is interesting."

Dulce's body quivered, then she slumped. Using so much magic when she wasn't used to it drained a person.

"That's great. Let's head back in." They stood, but once in the classroom Betsy placed a hand on her arm. "Kafi, can you inform Marco I'm going to check on the group in Germany. I want to bring Dulce. Her second proficiency is sensing and she's starting to figure things out. It could be a real help."

Trinity's head popped up. "Can I join you? I think I have sensing, and I'd like to learn what Mom's learning."

Violet leaned over to give her a hug. "I'll see you tonight. Where is tomorrow's press conference? Are the hours insane?"

"Gah! We're going to be in Tokyo. It's at three in the afternoon local time, which is one in the morning Wisconsin time. So, we either nap or don't sleep tonight and just sleep in tomorrow. My vote is the second." Betsy shrugged.

"Oh, yeah, I remember. I blocked that for a reason." She kissed Violet one more time. "I'll call before dropping in tonight and we can decide then."

Violet headed out and Betsy pulled up the email from the German group. She arranged for them all to meet at a park in a half hour. Then she directed Dulce and Trinity to get some food, put on their earpieces, and meet her out in the courtyard.

Betsy used Kafi's panel to make sure there was a landing spot, and then the three of them transported. They arrived at the German park a bit early.

It was a bit cooler in the park, and the grass was wet. "It looks like we just missed the rain."

Trinity looked around them. "We should head to a bar."

Dulce scoffed. "You're too young."

Before they could continue, a group of eleven people walked up to them. A male with short dark hair, dark eyes, and a wide smile stepped forward. "Speak German?"

Betsy had brought seven earpieces. The email hadn't been clear on how many would be needed and she figured it would be enough for communication. She handed one to the man and then said, "Dies wird Ihnen helfen, uns zu verstehen." She pointed to her ear and then both Dulce's and Trinity's ears.

He smiled. "Thank you." He took it and started putting it in his ear.

Dulce leaned forward. "I don't get it. You said that it would help him to understand us in English, why did he understand?"

"I didn't use English. I know German ... or a bit. It's rusty, but it's something I spoke at one time in my life."

Her hand flew to her ear and her eyes widened. "Oh! It translated you. Do you normally speak English?"

"Dulce, you rarely wear that when we talk." Betsy winked at her, answering her question of what language the two spoke in.

She blushed and giggled. Betsy wanted to roll her eyes but didn't.

"Hi, my name is Pascal. Thank you for traveling here, though I'm not really sure how you did it. Were you in the area?"

Betsy held out her hand. "Hi, I'm Betsy, this is Dulce and her daughter Trinity, and it's our pleasure to meet you." She stepped back once he let go of her hand. "Please, tell me your story."

"Well, we each have a story of fire happening when and where it shouldn't. We figure that's a form of magic." As he spoke, Betsy handed out the remaining earpieces. "It started at my home, but then when I spoke to my wife, Yvette," he indicated a woman in the crowd, "she told me her friends had told her similar stories had happened to them. We all decided to contact your website."

When Betsy closed her eyes, the group didn't register as anything but human to her. She turned to Dulce. "So, what do you think?"

"Me?"

"Well, yes. This is why I brought you. What are you sensing?"

Both mother and daughter shut their eyes. Then Trinity smiled. "They aren't like my friends, or the people at magic school. I started doing something like this before you came to Colorado. But they aren't like us. They're ... something. Different. I can't explain it."

Betsy sighed. "I think I can." She shook her head realizing these people must be like the people of Oz, witches. Her to-do list was growing longer every day, not shorter. "I think we have to change the website."

"Why?" Though Trinity asked, everyone with an earpiece gaped at her, realizing something was very different.

"Because there are two types of magic. One is so rare, most beings in the galaxy don't even know about it. The other is what I am ... a wizard." She looked at the group of Germans. "I believe Earth may be something new in the galaxy in many many ways."

Pascal's brow furrowed. "Does that mean you can't help us?"

"Oh, I believe I can. Though this is a different way to access magic than I do and although most beings in the galaxy don't know about it, *we* know about it. Securing a teacher for you will be a top priority and one that shouldn't be impossible."

14

*There Isn't Enough Coffee In The World ... Literally*

Betsy

Betsy and Violet had an early dinner, then opted for a nap. The alarm woke them just before midnight and Betsy debated throwing the clock across the room. She'd had it for years, but the idea of the sound of it crashing into bits brought her joy.

"Morning, my storm cloud." Violet leaned over to give Betsy a kiss.

"I really am a storm cloud right now. Morning, sunshine." As awful as the interrupted sleep was, waking with Violet almost made it worth it.

They both got up and ready. In the kitchen, Betsy ordered coffee and two hot ham and cheese sandwiches from the panel. She was too tired to cook. Once they'd eaten, she dialed up the transport location in Tokyo, and they were off.

Betsy's body tingled with fatigue. She'd gotten sleep, and the window she looked out of in the room she landed in told her it was a sunny day in Japan, but her body begged for bed. Her mind felt like mush and her muscles were wobbly.

The theory of doing press conferences at three in the afternoon local time was great, but if she wasn't traveling to the area for several days, it would be impossible to acclimate. But she was too busy to spend each week on location.

Violet grabbed her arms and rotated her so they faced each other. "Are you okay, love?"

"Yeah ... mostly." Betsy shook her head. "I just feel a bit like I've been hit by a truck. I should be fine once they're asking their questions. Let's go."

Though Violet didn't respond, Betsy saw the concern in her expression.

They headed off to find the cameras.

Before they got there, hair and makeup found them, got them pretty, and sent them to the table on the stage.

Once they were seated with a mug of coffee, Violet leaned over and whispered, "Did the makeup person say the bags under your eyes had bags and ask if they were going on a trip?"

Betsy smiled. "Yep. I told her that's how I managed the one piece of checked luggage on the plane."

Violet laughed.

As the room filled, Betsy finished her coffee and her head began to clear. *You can do this! You've done a lot of things half asleep.*

Despite being in a new location, each conference had a similar feeling. Cameras, lots of people, and a small stage for her and Violet to sit on, behind a table, with microphones. To the side was an MC who played to the crowd, giving introductions and asking questions when the mass of people didn't have any. So far, the attendees had plenty.

"Welcome, Tokyo! I am Sato Haru, and I'll be your host for today. We have Pillar Doeth and

Major North. After the number of press conferences they've done, I'm guessing we can just get things started. Pillar Doeth?"

Her accent was there, but she got the words out so clearly, Betsy was convinced she actually spoke English versus the earpiece translating it. "Hi. Once again, we're thrilled to be here. I would rather spend the time addressing questions you may have instead of using it on my own agenda. That said, I do have one announcement."

There was a murmur in the room and Betsy waited a few seconds while they discussed their predictions. She smiled. "In a recent encounter with some magic users, we realized it would be easier for all of you if we put some more guidelines on our website to help you determine if you or some of your loved ones have magic. There are two ways to access magic, to use the magic within or manipulate that around us. Throughout the galaxy, the wizards ... or Pillars, only use the magic from within. This second version of magic use is almost unheard of throughout the planets."

Sato Haru smiled. "Is this second type of magic less honorable than what you do, Pillar Doeth?"

"No. Not at all." She shook her head quickly. "It's just different. And Earth has such a thick layer of magic around it, I'm not surprised that we're the ones with two styles. But we can discuss this more later. For now, expect to see what you need for self-testing on the website. Or if in any way you've begun to feel different and strange occurrences happen around you, that will be indication enough. Anyway, we're working with an IT expert to get the changes up as soon as possible."

A hand shot up from the audience and Betsy pointed. "We've heard that people in some areas are disappearing. Have you found any of them?"

Her body tensed as she thought about Dulaine and the others. "No. It's a high priority and we have done a few different approaches to search. There are more, and they are going to be used in the coming days."

"I don't understand. Why didn't you use them before?" Though his face stayed as neutral as his body, Betsy didn't need sensing magic to read his intention of chaos.

"Sir, the Earth is a large place. We can't just throw a spell that will cover ... well, everything. We need to narrow our search to a smaller area. After the extensive work of the last week, we have some new data coming in that has allowed us to find areas that we can focus on. That is what we'll do next. Magic doesn't mean we can do things instantly; it's just one more tool."

His eyes narrowed and she wondered if he had more to say, but then he let himself sit heavily in his seat.

A young girl with large dark eyes and black hair raised her hand. Betsy wasn't sure why her look stood out in a room where most of the people shared similar characteristics, but there was something about her. Lifting her hand, she waved her fingers to indicate she should speak.

The girl stood and nodded. "Where is the qynad?" Her voice was airy and high pitched. Once she was done, she gave a slight bow.

Betsy smiled and tried to look nice ... or at least unthreatening. "Xantay wouldn't fit in this room. Though it is big, not quite big enough for a creature of her stature. That said, we may be able to set up more appearances with her if you have any questions."

"I just wanted to know how she spoke my language. Do all qynad speak like me?" Her eyes widened and hope poured from her.

Betsy took a moment to let her question sink in. She knew the concept of a beast that looked like a dragon from legend, speaking, had rocked social media. When she'd spoken to Xantay, she'd been pleased.

"When Xantay agreed to partner with me at the last press conference, we knew that communication would be an issue. Major North has learned a couple of Earth languages, including English. If you notice, during these sessions, we don't have a translator with us. We do, however, have these earpieces. Despite them, we don't wait for someone to translate before answering. That's because the programming in this is sophisticated enough to translate any language to what the listener understands automatically."

As Betsy spoke, the girl's face contorted in confusion. For a moment, her jaw tightened. Then Betsy took a breath. "We set up the room in Dubai with a combination of technology and magic so that anyone who was in there would hear the answers in their own language. It worked as we spoke, so even people watching over the internet would experience their own language."

The angry man who'd asked the first question shot back to his feet. "That's impossible. There is no way that you could've done that! Not without—"

"Magic?" Betsy interrupted.

His eyes bulged.

She lifted both her hands. "The thing is that the basic technology of the earpieces isn't difficult—"

"And how much are you going to charge us for the *privilege* to have a set?" he snapped, his accent getting thicker the more his frustration bubbled up.

"The ability to communicate is fundamental to understanding each other. The specs for the earpiece I am wearing will be uploaded to the internet. Anyone can create a program that can be included in current phone technology. We want the availability to be universal. If we had the ability, we'd give the earpieces out to everyone, we just don't have the means to do it quickly enough. That said, we will be taking action on any company that tries to make a profit on the technology."

Sato Haru leaned in. "Would your group be offering any incentives for companies willing to produce these at high volume and hand them out for free."

"Yes," Violet declared next to her. "In a joint effort with the chanzii, I believe this offer can be made."

Betsy nodded at her enthusiasm. "The actual materials aren't expensive and the programming is done. All that is left is production. We all know that most companies put things out at a huge profit. We will find a way to bring this to the people. It may be working with the government or giving tax breaks, but we'll find a way."

15

*A Picnic In The Park*

## Pearl

The store was full of people. Pearl wasn't sure if the townsfolk were stockpiling because they were worried or if it was just a busy Friday, but the apothecary was packed.

The bell rang and she looked up with a smile, ready to greet the next customer. "Mom! When did it get to be so late?"

Mom looked around the store. "Well, if it's been this busy, I imagine the time slipped by while you worked. Is Dad in the back mixing orders?"

"Yep. He's been busy all day." She looked at her watch. "I still can't believe how late it is, but I should head out. You need me back at one? One-thirty? Monday?"

She laughed. "I was thinking of telling you to take the afternoon off, but if we continue to have this many customers, we'll need you for the afternoon rush, so yes, be back after lunch. Now, go enjoy your date."

Excitement bubbled within her as she thought about Marco and their scheduled lunch. "Mom, it's not a date. We're getting together to compare notes on what he and the other Pillars have done in their search for Dulaine. I'm also curious about the conferences and magic school. You *know* that." Then she thought of her usual Friday lunch date and her smile faltered. *I hope Dulaine is okay. She's been gone so long, I hope she knows we're all looking for her.* She sighed. There wasn't anything she could do right now.

"I know, you just have to realize that everything is being done to find your sister, but life does continue, and you and that boy are cute together."

She worked at keeping a blank face. "Okay, Mom. I'll see you later."

Enjoying the fresh air, she left the store and walked towards the edge of town. It was just before noon, and Marco said he'd meet her in the field outside the school at twelve. As excited as she was to see him, she'd give anything to be meeting Dulaine.

*Stop it Pearl. Worrying over her won't bring her back. You can fight once you have a target. If you spend all your time thinking about Dulaine, your life will go by without you living it. I have to continue to worry but also live. It's what she'd want.*

As she walked across the grass, Marco's solid form fazed in a few feet in front of her. His short black hair ruffled in the wind as he turned to face her. When his deep brown eyes met hers, a smile spread across his face, making him look like a kid in a candy store. Eyes twinkling, he said, "Nice timing. Or have you been waiting?"

"No, not waiting. I just arrived." She narrowed her eyes. "You knew that though, right? You told me that you always scan an area before you transport in. You checked that the field was empty, right?"

"You really are clever." He reached out and wrapped her hands in his. "I brought a picnic. Shall we eat?"

She smiled at him, tingles from his touch tickling throughout her body. "Sounds amazing."

Marco waved behind him and she saw a blanket and a basket. Working together, they spread out the blanket and sat. "I have sandwiches, chips, and water."

He handed out the food and asked about her week.

"It was good, outside of my constant worry for Dulaine. Everyone in town is working hard to find her and helping me and the family to not lose it. But if I'm honest, I keep wanting to find someone to fight to get Dulaine back."

He slumped. "I know what you mean. We're all searching. We each have a specialty and we're making sure she's a top priority for all of us. We're going to find her."

"Thank you." Pearl's eyes began to tear. She shook her head. "How's the training going? Have a lot of people been contacting you about magic?"

He chuckled. "I forget that all of you skip out on the press conferences."

"Well, not all of us. Devlin usually watches them, but wasn't the last one in the middle of the night?" She took a bite of her sandwich. The zesty flavors exploded in her mouth. "Wow! This is amazing."

"It was," he laughed, then sipped his water. "I stayed up to watch, then slept. I'm guessing if anything, Betsy is just getting up now. She probably had to answer questions for a good hour after it ended and then got home. I can't imagine being so ... vibrant in every time zone." He lifted his sandwich. "It's a Middle Eastern special with hummus, lamb, cucumber, tzatziki, and... other things."

"Well it's really good." Pearl imagined Betsy trying to keep up with sleep and all the different time zones and was amused. "So, tell me, what did I miss from this press conference?"

"We're locating more people all over the place who are doing magic like all of you. We're going to have to take lessons from Oz or find some teachers from among your people to bring back to our school."

Her jaw dropped. "Really? More witches? You're not just unearthing wizards? Are you finding more places where people knew they were doing magic?"

His brow creased. "No. And isn't that weird? You'd think there'd be others. If not full towns, then individuals."

"I would think that." She finished her meal and wiped her hands on a napkin. "So, what you're saying is, you need us to find volunteers willing to help you teach."

Her heart nearly melted as his nose scrunched up and he shrugged. She couldn't believe how quickly she was falling for this Pillar. "Well, yes. Kind of."

"You're a dork. Once we're done, let's talk with Devlin and then my Mom. I'm sure we can find some people."

His face transformed from an errant boy trying to get his way to a beautiful man as a smile bloomed on his face. "Great, but first, I brought cookies."

16

## *An Old Friend*

### Betsy

The Ziner had made it to Earth's orbit, so despite it being Saturday, Violet was busy. Betsy sat on a pool chair in her yard drinking a lemon-blueberry smoothie. Wes and Buttercup alternated between flying in circles above her and disappearing into the woods. It made her happy to know they enjoyed her property.

So far, her program had picked up a few hits. She started with having people on Juk's team follow up on the leads. Betsy was one person; she couldn't be everywhere. Though she relaxed now,. this afternoon, once everyone on the Ziner were settled, Betsy planned on meeting up with Violet and Horax, or whoever commanded the ship, and discussing their plans for their stay.

*If the ship can do a planet-wide search for Dulaine, maybe we can find her more quickly. Can they search for a specific person?*

As she finished her shake, she debated if she wanted another one, or something else. *Maybe coffee ... or real food.*

With a sigh, she forced herself to stand and move around. She knew she had to have more than a smoothie.

Sitting on the steps to her door, leaning back on his hands, face tipped up to the sun with a smile on his face, sat Balzeno. The dwarf exuded calm with both ven sleeping next to him.

Betsy massaged her temples. *How long has he been here? Why didn't he let me know when he arrived?*

He was an Elder, she couldn't yell at him, even if she wanted to. She liked him, he was one of her favorite Elders, but he tended to pop up unannounced more than the others. She'd like a warning, maybe just once.

"Welcome to my home, Elder."

The only reaction he gave to hearing her was a slight twitch to the left side of his mouth.

After taking a slow breath, she walked around him into the house. She left the door open, a sign he was free to follow her. She began to prepare mac and cheese, a dish that was hard to find off of Earth.

She had four cheeses to add to the sauce and some leftover barbecue brisket she mixed into the full casserole before covering with a breadcrumb topping and broiling in the oven.

On the side, she put together a salad.

Just as everything was coming together, Balzeno lumbered in. "It smells great in here. You didn't do all of this for me, did you?"

"Of course I did. I was hungry myself, but decided I wanted to cook for you, too." She smiled as he sat at the table. "I wasn't sure if you'd had baked mac and cheese."

They both ate a few bites, then he moaned in appreciation. "This is amazing, Pillar Doeth, but tell me, don't all Earthlings have vegemite on their table?"

She grunted but got up and found the jar she'd purchased for Violet.

After adding the awful condiment to her perfect meal, Balzeno leaned back and patted his belly. "I do hope you'll let me take some of this home with me. It may be one of the best things I've had in a while."

"Thank you for the compliment, and of course." She cleared the dishes. "So, what are you doing here? Is there something I can help you with?"

His eyes narrowed on her and his smile slowly spread across his face. "It's been some time since I've had a relaxing day on a planet. Do you mind us sitting outside?"

"Not at all."

Out in the sun, relaxed, Betsy realized there was something different about the dwarf. She wasn't sure what it was, but it had been there since she noticed him on her stoop. A breeze whipped her hair, and a chill traveled down her back before she decided her mind was playing tricks on her.

Balzeno lifted his head up towards the sky again, and his face softened.

"Would you like to sit by the pool or maybe walk through the woods?"

Wes darted between them and the trees, twisting and twirling in the air. Buttercup drifted more slowly, letting them know she agreed that she wanted them to join them in the woods.

Laughing, Balzeno waved his hand. "Apparently, the rascals of the air have decided for us. Lead on, Pillar."

The two headed into the cool shade of the trees, following the path that circumnavigated her property.

Balzeno sighed. "I've spent too much time lately on ships and space stations. It's nice to breathe fresh air."

"Did you complete what you needed to back on your planet?"

"I only got as far as Torville Station Number Six. I can create a private line home from there." His face scrunched up. "At least, they say it's private. I've always wondered how private it really is. From what I understand, it's not dwarven technology."

Betsy laughed and shook her head. The arrogance of all Elders was beyond unprecedented.

Just because they were good with three magical proficiencies didn't mean they were all knowing.

Their path opened up and they could see the ven darting back and forth above them. Balzeno, who probably had abilities in all magical proficiencies, lifted a hand and created a yellow ball for the flying creatures to play with.

She narrowed her eyes. "Is that just light? Is there any substance to it? It won't start a fire, will it?" Betsy wasn't sure why she worried with his skill level, but it made her nervous.

"Oh, don't worry." There was laughter in his voice. "It is energy based, but I gave it a bit of oomph. The kiddos up there should be able to play with it without any issues."

As she watched, the two furry beasts began swatting at the ball with their paws. The yellow light ball flew back and forth, and the ven made sounds of ecstatic happiness.

Her focus continued to follow the air antics as she asked, "So, you've been given official permission to be assigned here?"

"Yes. Now I just need to find a place to live until that home of mine is built."

Betsy shook her head. "I'm thinking we should adjust your location. I want to speak with people of Oz and bring some of them to Pillar Owusu's school in Africa. I think it may be safer." A large sigh escaped her. "Have you heard that Dulaine was taken?"

"I have. Pillar Kor told me before we traveled here."

"Viera's here?"

"You didn't know?"

Hope blossomed in Betsy. "I didn't. News doesn't travel fast between worlds. I'm so relieved. We should—"

A crash above her interrupted her thoughts. She looked and found the top of a dead tree was on fire and she didn't see the two ven anywhere.

Thoughts of her woods burning and the flames possibly reaching her home twisted her gut. Her hands shot up and she imagined the air around the tree reforming. *Air is made of oxygen, and there is hydrogen in there as well. If I just ... remix. Two hydrogen, one oxygen ...*

Water formed around the fire in a small, suspended pool, putting out the flame before it could hop to the next tree. For a moment, her muscles relaxed and she breathed a sigh. Then the heat from the area flowed over her and she realized the fire could still reignite. Clenching her jaw, she imagined depressurizing the area around the tops of the trees until the air spoke to her.

Her ears popped as she released her spell.

Frustrated, she turned to Balzeno. "I told you not to do anything that could create fire!" Her earlier decision not to yell at the Elder flew out the door.

Despite her anger, Balzeno gazed at her, his face blank. He acted as if more intrigued with what she'd do next than contrite with the fire he'd started.

The sharp pain of her nails biting into her palms with her anger brought down some of her fury and she realized she needed to release some emotion. From an old habit, she created a dirt arrow, and with a flip of her wrist, shot it at the dead tree with the air manipulation Zuza had taught her years ago.

The fear she'd felt at the trees burning down amped up the spell to the point the projectile blew a hole straight through the dead trunk. "What the hell?" she whispered.

Slightly humming, Balzeno sauntered over to the tree. "Nice aim, Pillar Doeth. You combined solid and air, did you not?"

The roiling temper dissipated as she watched him trace the hole with a practiced finger. Then he straightened and narrowed his gaze on her. "And how did you put out the fire I accidentally set? Which, I am sorry for setting."

Her mind was a jumble. *How did I put it out? All I know is that I didn't want an escaped flame in my woods.* "Um, I guess I created water? Does that make sense? Or was it depressurizing the area? It all happened so fast."

"That it did, young one." One eyebrow raised and his mouth quirked, Balzeno asked, "Where did those pesky ven get off to?"

With a grunt, Betsy shut her eyes. Her life magic worked better when beasts were on land and she could amplify with feeling them through the earth, but she could sometimes feel life if the animals were in trees. "I ... well, I think their wing beats are making a lot of noise to the south, maybe a half-mile away."

She shook her head, not sure she was making any sense.

"Very good, Pillar Doeth. Your elevation is complete." There was a joy in his voice she couldn't place. With everything else, Betsy decided she'd figure it out later. For now, fire, ven, and her woods were a higher priority.

"My what? Never mind. We need to get back to my house. I need to speak with Viera about finding Dulaine. I can't believe we're taking a walk when you knew our best chance of finding the girl had returned to Earth with you." She turned and stomped off.

"I agree she's our best help, but she won't be available yet, she's still waking up and getting her feet under her."

17

## *Task Force*

### Betsy

The cool shadows of the woods helped to calm Betsy after the near fire Balzeno accidentally set. They hadn't gotten too far in their walk before the weird event, and the more she thought about it the more it didn't make sense. Balzeno was too old to be making these kinds of mistakes.

She decided she'd ask him about it once she figured out exactly why the whole situation rubbed her wrong. For now, there were bigger things to worry about. She needed to focus on Dulaine.

They'd returned to her home, standing just outside the door. She wanted to get to the Athletic Center in the chanzii subdivision or Violet's house and see if whomever was commanding the Ziner was around. Even if Viera wasn't available, the Ziner's tech should be helpful and more sensitive than anything they'd used so far.

*If they can do a sweep of the planet for hot spots of potential wizards, it could give us places to hone our searches. That would help either Zuza or Viera with their magic.*

Balzeno tucked his thumbs in his waistband and rocked back on his heels. "Well, I think I'm going to head down to Oz, if you don't mind. It has been lovely catching up with you. But I'd like to speak with the family."

Betsy's jaw dropped, but then she snapped it shut. "Would you like me to contact Pearl first?"

"Oh, I don't think that will be necessary. I'll just mosey around until I find one of the people I've met. I'm sure it'll be fine." He winked, tapped at his wrist, then was gone.

She felt the tension building within her. That Elder was going to be trouble. It was weird because she'd always considered Balzeno one of the more agreeable of the Elders. Was this a sign of things to come? Was he going to cause more trouble than be helpful?

Betsy shut her eyes and did a few breathing exercises, willing the serenity of her land to infuse her and relax her body. The earth filled her with strength as a breeze washed away some of her stress.

Above, Wes and Buttercup returned, making sounds of pleasure, mirroring her own better mood. "Okay, rascals. Let's go inside and get some things done."

After a quick stop in the kitchen to fill a mug of tea, she headed up to her home office to check her computer. While the program ran a report, she contacted the Ziner.

"Horax here. How can I help you, Pillar Doeth?"

A smile spread on her face. "Horax! It's great to hear from you. Have you checked in with Xantay or anyone else on planet?"

"I have. After speaking with Major North, I spoke to Mr. Hopkins and of course my daughter."

His voice softened a bit at the end. "I assume she's been representing herself and the qynad well."

"She has. You can even watch the press conference she attended." There was a small gasp at that. "She was amazing."

"That's great, thank you for letting me know." There was a pause. "Is there anything else, Pillar Doeth?"

A part of her wanted to demand he call her Betsy, but he wasn't because he was on the bridge of the ship, she was sure. "How is Viera?"

"Oh, she's good. She woke up and was tired. She needs to eat and get over being in that box."

Betsy shook her head, confused. "Box?"

"You'll have to get the details from Balzeno."

A spike of annoyance at the Elder shot through her again, but then she sighed. "Will do."

"Anything else?" His gravelly voice made her smile.

"I was just wondering if you could do a sweep of the planet looking for clusters of wizards."

There was a pause before he said, "We can, but the results won't be very specific, or fast. This ship doesn't have that technology, so we'll have to cobble together the sensors to bend to our will. I mean, I'm good, I can do it, but not as well as with a different ship. We can do a fast search and get you the results today, but that will only give you areas about the size of full states or maybe small countries. If you can wait, we can narrow it down. Maybe give you better answers over the next few days."

"That would be amazing." Relief washed through her.

"Then that's what I'll do," he promised.

Betsy signed off and checked her program. The outcomes weren't what she'd hoped. The problem was people weren't looking for, finding, and selling magic users on the black web—at least, not yet. Wanting to punch the code, she spent a few minutes refining it a bit but then saw she had a message from Zuza.

On a whim, she called him. "Betsy, you're available."

"I am. You mentioned you found a spot you think they're holding humans with magic?"

He grunted. "A woman went to the police here in London. A friend of mine on the force contacted me. Her friend was visiting Dubai with a group. The friend texted that she was going to call one of the numbers on a flier. The woman here in London told her friend to use our website, but the woman in Dubai didn't want to wait for someone in the government to contact her. They compromised, and she put one of those electronic suitcase locator devices in her bra. The problem came when the device stopped working. Long story short, we have somewhere to start. We have a general location when it stopped working, but nothing more."

"Okay, that's good, I think. I don't think we'll find Dulaine in Dubai, but I'd love to finally close down one of these groups." She sipped her tea. "I think we should bring Pearl. She isn't trained, but she's in her twenties, knows a lot, and has magic. Even though her sister won't be there, she wants to be involved. The sooner she starts, the better."

There was a pause. "Okay, but it's seven right now, so ten in Dubai. I don't want to wait much longer."

Betsy checked her watch: one. *I need to grab a bit more to eat if we're off to use magic. Brunch with Balzeno was good but not enough.* "I agree. Though, I don't know when it got to be so late. It's afternoon already? Gah!" Betsy shook her head.

"Either way, give me a place to meet you, and I'll be there in half an hour."

"Sounds good."

Betsy patted her pockets and found the jade stone Devlin had given her. She still felt like a fool using it, but she always kept it on her. With a bit of intent, activating it to make the stone more than it was, creating a link between her and her target, she said, "Pearl?"

It didn't take long for Pearl's voice to come back through the gem. "Betsy?"

Amusement washed through her at the idea of speaking through a small green rock. "I don't know if you're busy, but Zuza found a compound in Dubai with humans with magic we believe are being held against their wishes. He and I are going in to investigate and if needed, break it up. There is a good chance that Dulaine won't be there. I want you to understand that. I'm extending an invitation to you to join us ... if you really want to be part of this fight. The thing is, you'll have to trust our transport."

There was a pregnant pause, then a sigh. "Yes. Just ... tell me where."

"Don't you need me to come and pick you up?"

She laughed a bit awkwardly. "Marco is here. He signaled that he could bring me. We just need to know where."

"Marco, you toad." She laughed. "Can I text or do I need to call? Oh, wait, Zuza sent me the coordinates." She relayed them to Marco via Pearl. "See you two soon. We're going in with or without you. Don't dally."

That said, Betsy dashed to her room to change into jeans and to throw on a thicker shirt. Then she put on her dad's double chain phoenix hair woven bracelet. She didn't always have it on, but it did help to amplify her magic. She knew the danger of always wearing the imbued item, so she was careful about how often she wore it.

Where Viera seemed to have found three imbued items, she just had the one. At the end of the day, the bracelet was all she really wanted.

*I love you, Dad. Thank you for always watching over me.*

Back down in the kitchen, she grabbed a protein bar, then she checked the touchdown spot, saw it was clear, and dialed the transport.

Zuza was the last to arrive. When he saw Marco, he chuckled. "I see we may have a chance at a new generation, yet."

Both Marco and Pearl blushed, but neither denied it. *Interesting.*

"Okay, team." Zuza smiled at them. "I had Xantay use the shuttle to search this location. That small ship couldn't do a full planet search, but with her programming and a restricted area to search, she's brilliant."

"Agreed." Marco said.

"She confined the scope to about three square blocks." Zuza continued. "I'm going to use my sense to narrow it down more. It'll take me a couple of minutes."

Betsy, Pearl, and Marco watched over him as he shut his eyes. Betsy felt the power as his magic seemed to blanket the area around her.

Zuza gasped, then shook his head. "I don't know how much more I'll be able to do, magically, after that. The group isn't very close. If we'd landed nearer to them, it wouldn't have used as much of my reserve. Gods, I wish Viera weren't indisposed."

Marco perked up. "Viera's back?"

"Yeah, but from what I understand, she won't be available to help until sometime later tonight or tomorrow." Zuza shrugged. "Anyway, let's go that way." He pointed and they all walked for a couple of blocks. "I believe they're in one of these two buildings."

Betsy closed her eyes and held up her hands. She used a combination of life and solid, but she'd been using magic all day and was tired. "It's the one on the left." She sounded tired, even to herself.

Next to her, Marco was in a similar position. He shook his head. "Yeah, I agree. When will I be as fast at these proficiencies as you, Pillar Doeth?"

She slapped his arm. "I'm like four times older than you. Maybe when you're not a baby?"

"Closer to five times older, but you know, old brains ..." He ducked, and Zuza led them towards the building waving his hand to motion them to silence.

As they had been joking and doing their magic, Pearl smiled but seemed more awe struck than anything else.

Marco put his hand on the door handle, twisted, and the door silently opened.

"Wasn't the door locked?" Pearl spoke softly, but if anyone was in the room, she would've been heard.

Marco nodded. "Yes, but I disintegrated the metal locks. It's hard to keep out someone with magic. Now, this room is empty, and I think the rest of the building above is as well. I'm only picking up the wizards in a basement, but in case I'm missing something, let's keep quiet."

Eyes wide, Pearl's mouth opened a bit and she nodded her understanding.

The door opened to a receptionist's area.

Betsy spoke low. "I agree, all indications of life are below. We need to find stairs."

They headed through the only door and Marco shut his eyes with his hand on a wall. He whispered. "There's something on the other end of the hall."

They walked softly to the end. There were two doors. Zuza carefully opened each door. Behind the first was a lab. The second was a restroom. He shut his eyes and traced his hand along the wall with the restroom, then pushed. A panel the size of a double door unfolded, revealing an opening that led to a dark hole.

Pearl tapped them on the shoulder and waved them back.

Zuza closed the hidden door, and they retreated back down the hall to the main room they entered into.

"I have a tincture that will help us see better in the dark. I wasn't sure what we'd need but figured seeing in the dark may be helpful. I have a half dozen of these." She held up two bottles. After Marco and Zuza took them, she pulled out two more.

Betsy drank the liquid and the building looked almost day bright. *I have to learn this imbuing magic!*

Back at the stairs, the void of black was still dark, but navigable. Once they got to the bottom, they found five people chained to beds. They weren't moving. Betsy moved up to the first. The others each moved to beds as well. In the back of her mind Betsy remembered Pearl had a medical degree and Marco was better with medical magic than she was.

Marco said, "Alive, just drugged."

Betsy searched the room. "Is this all of them?"

Zuza closed his eyes. After a moment he nodded. "From what I can tell, yes. We can have another swipe done once we have these people taken to safety." He tapped his wrist. "Horax, can you clear everyone from this room? We have five people drugged and chained to beds and four of us. Can we be moved to the African school?"

"We can do that, but we have a full medical team on the Ziner. Would you like to start here?"

He looked at Betsy and Marco who both nodded.

"We'd be happy to take you up on that offer."

## 18

## *Lost Sister*

### Pearl

We found a bunch of people held by a group who Zuza thinks were up to no good. As much as I'm excited to have helped them, Du-Drop isn't one of them. I checked them all.

*Where is she? Where is my sister?*

Pearl worked to keep tears from sliding down her face. She knew Dubai was probably too far for her sister ... but she'd hoped. She sniffed, trying to be brave.

The air smelled clean for being canned and recycled.

*I'm on a ship.*

The medical staff were aliens. Though most were like Violet, turquoise with purple hair, but there were others as well.

*I'm on a spaceship ... like, in space.*

Pearl's body trembled as she pushed herself into the corner. Her breathing got choppy.

"I think this is the woman's friend from London. We've found a luggage tracker on her." Zuza sounded excited to have identified one of the five.

Betsy looked through the faces of missing people from a site someone had set up. "This is the man's sister who yelled at me and Violet in Dubai during our press conference. I'm glad we found her. Now we just need to identify these other three people, then find all the other missing people."

*I agree, especially if Du-Drop is top of the list.* Pearl's jaw tightened as she stood to the side of the medical suite on a ship in space. Her mind could barely register everything that happened, but she had to focus on what she felt was important, her sister. *That isn't fair, to only care about Dulaine, I know the others matter too, but she's so much younger than any of these people ... and she's my sister.*

As she watched the people getting care, she wanted to help but feared she wouldn't be enough. She knew medicine, even some spells. Her body froze.

*Don't use magic ... what if you bring the whole thing down ... where would it go? To Earth? The moon? The sun?*

She shivered as the idea played out in her mind. Different ways the ship could be destroyed seemed to repeat like a film reel as the five people they had rescued were tended to.

As she watched, Betsy gazed at her, then looked towards Marco, her face tightening. One of Betsy's eyebrows rose, then Marco sighed and nodded. "Right," he mumbled under his breath.

*Can they talk to each other mind to mind?* Pearl tore her attention from them and stared at the patient being helped on the other side of the room. *Are they talking about me? Am I doing something wrong? Is Marco mad at me? Will they send me away?*

"Hi." Marco's deep voice jerked her from her spiraling thoughts. "You okay?"

"I'm ... yeah, of course I am. I mean, I'm on a spaceship ... in space. Why wouldn't I be okay?" She could feel her pulse beat in her neck.

His smile made her breath hitch. "Do you want to tour the ship? We could head to the cafeteria and get something to eat."

"Shouldn't we stay here? Isn't your magic a healing magic? Are you needed? Am I in the way?" *Am I babbling?*

He slid an arm over her shoulder. "Come on. Let's go see what we can find."

Pearl let him lead her out of the medical suite. Once they got into the hall, she thought her head may explode. It was all so ... advanced: technical, sleek, and well, alien.

Marco dragged a finger over the black mirror-like paneling that tiled the top half of the hexagonal hallway wall and part of it flared to life. "These panels access the computer. They are voice and text accessible, kind of like our phones, though the voice activation is more successful. Go ahead, tap one of the panels and ask for directions to the cafeteria."

"What? Really?" She couldn't believe what he asked of her.

"Yep. I want to show you how easy it is to interact with the panels so that you'll feel more empowered." He leaned down to kiss her cheek.

"What about my magic and bad luck with electronics?"

He smirked, waggling his eyebrows. "I'd suggest not using your magic while you ask for directions."

Her hands were moist and she wiped them on her thighs. Licking her lips, she stepped up to the wall, then tapped the black part with her pointer-finger. It lit up and she smiled, feeling like she accomplished something. "Um, could you please tell me how to get to the cafeteria?"

A metallic voice emitted from the wall and lights flashed indicating the direction, but Pearl was lost. Everything was in symbols and characters that meant nothing to her. The voice spoke in a language she didn't know. Eyes wide, she looked at Marco and shrugged.

"You forgot your earpiece translator." He laughed. "Here, take mine. Most people will speak Galactic Standard, and I know it."

"Are you sure?" She bit her lip.

"I am."

She slipped the device on, and they headed in the direction the lights indicated. Though there weren't many creatures in the hallways, there were a few, and they were all ... fantastic. When they arrived at an elevator, Marco took over, tapping the controls in a manner she didn't follow. In the small box, she looked up at him. "Is this thing moving? It feels like it's broken."

"Not broken." He slid his hand into hers. "So, now that we're alone. Are you really okay?"

"Yes, why do you keep asking?"

The doors opened, and they continued to follow the lights. "Because, Pearl, you were projecting images of the ship exploding in awful ways back in the medical bay. It worried Betsy."

"But not you?" Then his words sank in. "You two can read my mind?"

"And me. And no." His head shook fast. "We can pick up thoughts that you think loudly ... and those were some pretty loud thoughts."

They reached their destination and Pearl couldn't breathe. The room was full of ... *oh, my god.*

Marco rubbed her back. "They're all friends, Pearl. You've met other qynads, and though the ones here are bigger, they're still friends. There are phoenixes on the ship, but again, they are nice. Though, you probably won't interact with them; they are very introverted. The others, you may meet them, but maybe not. It all depends on the amount of time we spend up here."

"What about the ... um, Bigfoot-looking ... person?"

"Oh, the fing? They're the cooks ... at least the ones on the Ziner. They're really good in the kitchen. Not all of them. Like every species, they do everything, but the ones that I've met who cook are fantastic. I don't know how this ship secured a full complement."

"And—"

"How about we leave the doorway and go and sit down." Once again, he rubbed her back. The motion felt good and she breathed more easily.

Pearl allowed him to guide her. It wasn't until they got to the table that she realized she recognized the person sitting there. "I know you," she blurted.

The woman smiled up at her. "Yes, you do. Hi, Marco. Pearl, right? I'm Viera if you don't remember. I was on stage and then in that meeting with you that day. I take it you are less angry with all of us?" Her eyes narrowed. "And a bit overwhelmed. Trust me, that I understand. Sit, join me. Be at peace."

Something within Pearl relaxed and she finally took a full breath. She sat across from the only other Earthling in the room. "Yes. I've learned a lot. Though, I thought you'd gone to a different planet. Did you change your mind?"

Viera chuckled. "Sorry." She waved a hand. "I didn't realize how much I miss talking with another Earthling." She sighed. "No, I came back to help find," her eyes narrowed and she waved a finger towards Pearl, "your sister?"

"Oh? You came back for Dulaine?" Pearl's eyes got misty and she wanted to hug the other woman. "You traveled across the galaxy for me and my family?"

"I did. When the krottel opened up my magic, they pushed their sensing proficiency into me. My sensing happens to be *really* good. I have a job lined up on Abritos, but they need to set up the school, and that will take some time. So, I prioritized returning."

Marco had been typing on another one of those black panels. He looked up at Viera. "How long did it take for you to get here?"

"It's just over a week. We only stopped at Torville Station Number Six for an hour or so. We picked up Balzeno, who put me in an imbued chamber that he said taught me Galactic Standard. He said by the time I get back to Abritos I'll know Chanziian as well."

"They have a language box?" Marco snorted. "Those dwarves, they think of everything. Well, not everything, but damn, a lot. Okay, let's test this out. Take out your earpiece."

Viera sighed but did as she was told. Pearl decided to follow suit. Then Marco began to spew out syllables that didn't make any sense at all. She put her earpiece back in.

Viera's eyes widened. "I like most of the food, but everyone on the station is obsessed with vegemite, it's weird." Her hands slapped over her mouth, then she lowered them. "What language was that? Is this? What am I speaking?"

Marco smiled. "Nice job. Apparently the box worked. Your Galactic Standard is good."

The other woman laughed. It sounded a bit manic, though she looked happy.

A light on the panel turned yellow, and Marco hopped up. "I'll be back."

Pearl watched him run off. "Where is he going?"

"He's grabbing the food he ordered. I'm guessing for both of you."

"Oh." Pearl smiled. "That's right ... cafeteria."

Betsy came up to their table. "Viera!" She circled to the other side and pulled Viera into a big hug. "It's great to see you. How do you like living on Abritos?"

Viera smiled, her face softening. "I love it. It's nice seeing friends though. My head may explode coming home so soon, but I want to start searching. Are there places you want me to start? What day is it? Time? I'm not even going to try to convert."

Betsy laughed. "You *could* check your phone, but if you must know, it's July twenty-seventh. You left June twenty-ninth. You've been gone for one month, my friend."

"Really? That's it? It feels like both a lifetime and only a few days." She picked up a mug of coffee and finished it. "Well, you have me for a few days, then I'm off again and you won't see me for longer than a month. I don't know if I'm built for all this travel."

Everyone laughed, and Pearl wondered why that was so funny. She thought crossing the galaxy over and over sounded tedious, too.

Betsy reached over and squeezed Viera's hand. "I never thought you'd go more than a couple of miles from home, my friend, and now you're traveling the galaxy, so no, I'm sure this is a lot for you."

Marco sat and handed Pearl something that looked like hot cereal with nuts and fruit ... but nothing looked familiar. She slowly took a bite, and it tasted fine.

"Tell me about tonight's rescue," Viera said.

Pearl's face scrunched up. "How did you know? We just arrived."

"Horax." Viera shrugged. "He's a big gossip."

The others chuckled at the comment.

With a shrug, Pearl just nodded. She didn't know who Horax was, but she figured if the others were amused, it must be true. She leaned forward. "Did you notice how easy it all was? Like, there weren't any guards. Do you think the other places will be so in-and-out and on our way?"

Marco placed his bowl down. While Pearl had only had about three bites, he was done. Apparently it didn't matter how old the twenty-year-old-looking male was. If he looked twenty, he ate in a flash. Or maybe it was all the magic he'd used.

He tapped his finger on the table, staring off into space. Finally, he focused on her. "I doubt it. I think they were particularly arrogant or dumb. They thought the location would be protection enough. That and the hidden stairs. My guess is, if and when we find other places there will be more security."

"That was pretty wild," Pearl admitted. "I don't know how Zuza found that. And he did it so fast."

The others said, "Magic," at the same time.

Betsy got up, taking Viera's mug, and returned with two coffees. "Okay, if Horax can find our locations, can you help us search for more of these places tomorrow? If we only have you for a few days, I want to take advantage of you as much as we can."

Viera nodded. "That's the plan."

Pearl narrowed her eyes. "Didn't Zuza say searching that area took up all his power? How much can you do?"

With a shrug, Viera lifted her coffee mug in salute. "Probably not more than five cities, but if Betsy bribes me with my favorite food ... sans Vegemite, I may be persuaded to push myself."

At the naming of the Australian spread, Betsy nearly fell from the bench, laughing.

19

## *A Game Of Whack-A-Mole*

### Betsy

Sunday morning ... Wisconsin time, all of the people had been returned to the local authorities of their own locations. They all agreed to let the people's own governments handle any questioning about how they ended up in that basement. They could get the reports later.

The only person that Betsy wanted to personally reconnect was the sister of the man who'd interrupted her press conference in Dubai. She personally escorted him to find his sister. She wanted to ensure he not only was reconnected with her, but that he knew she was instrumental in her rescue.

There was going to be a new press conference about the rescue, the man demanded it, but that wouldn't happen until his sister was well enough to face the cameras. If Betsy could arrange it, Zuza or Marco would be there.

Once that was done, she'd managed to get some sleep. As promised, once the Ziner's scan was done, Horax sent her a report. He found four spots in Europe with high concentrations of magic users.

She made some calls, then they all met at Zuza's place. Betsy brought Viera and Marco brought Pearl.

Zuza served a proper tea. In her opinion, it was a bit early, but he couldn't help himself. Despite the early hour, no one was complaining about the small sandwiches, cookies, or cakes.

Betsy paced while she ate, earning a glare from the host. "Horax sent us locations in London, Paris, France, Granada, Spain; and Berlin, Germany. Each location was narrowed down to about a three to four square block radius. He apologized for the lack of specificity. The speed we requested and the density of people in most of the areas the groups are using are making it harder to get better data."

Viera shrugged. "Between me and Zuza, we should get you close enough to be able to use life magic. I think what Horax has done is fine. The city itself would've probably been good enough, right Zuza?"

He nodded, but he'd lost a bit of color. Betsy wasn't sure if Viera knew how much better her sensing ability was to Zuza's. "Of course."

Once they'd eaten their fill and partaken of the tea, Betsy helped clean up. Zuza tried to say 'no,' but they'd been friends for too long.

The group stepped from the building and walked to catch the underground.

Though Viera *could* use her magic from anywhere in London, there was no reason when they had a smaller region to start from. Once they got where they wanted, she scrunched up her face and almost folded into herself, as if she were about to be punched in the face. Then Betsy felt her magic flow for barely a second.

The cool power stopped almost as fast as it started and then Viera started to walk. A block and a half later, she repeated the action. Then she walked a block, turned a corner, and continued for half a block. One last blast of her power and she sighed. "The gray building on the corner with the two people sitting on the stoop playing cards. They're guards."

Pearl stepped up and put a hand on Viera's shoulder. "Are you okay? That looked painful."

"No, not painful. Not really. It's just that I need to work on my control. I can either release just about everything or lock it all down. When my magic is out, I get a lot of information. There are a lot of people around. I was just bracing myself for the onslaught."

Zuza put a hand on her shoulder. "Maybe we could work together. I could probably tap into your well and direct the magic. Get the information without overwhelming either of us."

Viera's eyes widened. "Is that a thing? Because you know, I'd really like it to be a thing."

"There's only one way to find out, but I suggest we wait until Paris and our next stop. You've done enough for now."

Betsy nodded at Marco. "Okay, implant the suggestion of sleep."

"I am not good at this."

"I know. How often do you get to practice?" She winked at him, trying to be encouraging. "You know how to see into their mind. Just push the most relaxing thing out towards them. A nap, a warm cup of milk, a lecture on the finer aspects of astrophysics given by my grandfather."

Marco laughed, then relaxed. "Okay, I get it." His eyes narrowed, and Betsy could feel him probing out with life magic. His push of 'relax' was good, but not enough. The first man yawned and the second one razzed him.

"Not bad, try again."

He did. It was better, but not quite there.

"You should get a pet, like a puppy. If you can put a puppy to sleep when it's in a hyper mood, you can do anything."

Betsy focused on the men. *'Sleep.'*

They slumped. She heard one begin to snore. "Let's move before that sound wakes them both up."

Marco got to the door first and disintegrated the lock, silently gaining them entrance.

Once the door was shut, Marco sent out his life magic to find the group. He mumbled as he worked. This time they were upstairs, but there were four more guards. Two in a room off to the left. One with the prisoners ... a non-magical human spark in the room. One—

"Intruders, by the door!" a man yelled from the top of the stairs, stomping his way down.

"Fuck." Marco took the word from her mouth.

Pearl pulled a sheet of paper from her bag and ripped a piece from it.

Two men ran into the room from the left. "Where?" They had guns out swinging around the room, pointing everywhere.

Betsy waved a hand and the bullets within the weapons turned to metal dust.

"Right th—" The head of the man on the stairs swung back and forth and then his eyes widened. "What the hell?"

Betsy wasn't sure what Pearl did, but she was going to sit the girl down and figure it out.

One of the men to Betsy's left lowered his gun and scoffed. "Have you taken something? We were told no drugs on this job. Fucking sober up!"

"I haven't!"

The two turned and headed back the way they'd come.

Marco lifted his hands and focused on the man on the stairs. Suddenly, he sat, then lay down, sleeping.

Pearl turned to him. "Did you just put him to sleep?"

"Shhh." We all hushed her at once.

As quietly as we could, we moved up the steps. Marco led the way to the room. Betsy's magic informed her it held the people they were looking for.

Viera lifted her hand. "I can put up a time bubble."

Betsy shook her head. "No, you'll waste all your power. Let me go first."

"But—"

Zuza put a hand on Viera's shoulder. "She can't stop a bullet, but she can turn it to dust. I'll blow it away with a bit of wind. The guard in there can't touch her."

Face hard, Viera said, "Fine."

Betsy opened the door. A woman with a gun sat in a chair with the gun pointing at her. She flipped her hand back, sunk low, and unwound the gun to dust.

In the room, the man began to swear. "The fuck? How the hell? The gun was brand new, bitch! What did you do? You owe me a new one."

On the far side of the room, on a fireplace mantel, sat a rock. It wasn't exactly a rock, it was something decorative, but all Betsy cared about was that it was made from the Earth. She picked it up magically and tossed it at the man's head. Trading lessons with Zuza had been the best suggestion her dad had given for stretching their magical abilities. She didn't use all her force, and when the man fell, she didn't think she'd killed him.

The others seemed to have heard the thump because they walked around her into the room. There was a commotion of talking, but Betsy needed a few seconds to relax before she faced more people.

Squatting down she closed her eyes to refocus. She needed a moment to gather herself.

After several minutes, she found herself sitting in a park under a tree. Viera smiled down at her. "Nicely done. The ten people there were sent to Zuza's place. They'll head to the police station with him and then he'll come and meet us here."

"Where is here, exactly?"

Viera helped her up. "We're in Paris, our second stop. Eat a bar, recoup, and then we can get started."

"Yes, ma'am!" Betsy chuckled and followed her friend's advice.

They weren't actually far from the spot Horax had given them. When they got close, Zuza showed up. With a hand on Viera's shoulder, he used her magic to guide them to the next building. Betsy was impressed with this use of their magic.

It was dinner time and the magical wizards they sought all sat at a picnic table outside. This was very different from the last two situations. Zuza walked up and started speaking to them in French.

He returned. "Apparently, this group is exactly who and what they appear to be. They want to learn the magic organically. They don't like the idea of experts teaching them. They kindly told me to piss off."

Marco snarled, "Did they learn to cook by rubbing two sticks together?"

Zuza smiled. "Just like Betsy."

She slapped his arm, then laughed. "Okay, Spain next."

They had a very similar experience in Granada. A center with eight people, all happy with their situation. The difference was this time they took Marco's number. They promised to stay in contact with him. They wanted to do things on their own, but liked the idea of regular check-ins.

"Fine!" Betsy grumped. "I guess some of the compounds aren't as bad as the rest. But I still don't like the idea that they're practicing with things that can do so much damage without experts. I think we should monitor the Paris group, even from afar. It's dangerous to leave them completely on their own."

Zuza laughed as he contacted Horax to send them to Germany. It was the easiest way to transport as a group.

It was late by local standards, and by the time they found the center, though it was much earlier in Wisconsin, Betsy just wanted to sleep.

Marco placed a hand on the building. "From what I count, there are two people with magic in here and like, eight other people. So what, four guards for each magic user?"

"This can't be good." Viera mumbled. "This is the last stop of the day. Hold on." She waved her hand, and a bubble wavered over the building. "I'll be right back." Though they could see the bubble, it would be invisible to people who didn't know to look for it.

Betsy whistled. "You're getting good at those."

"Yeah, the cantankerous one has me practicing them a lot."

Betsy chuckled as Viera slipped into the bubble.

Pearl searched all their faces, clearly confused.

Marco rubbed her arm. "She threw up a time bubble, effectively stopping time for the people in the house. She can move in and out of the bubble since she has a time proficiency. It's almost as rare as imbuing. Once she's scoped everything out, she'll come back and report her findings."

It didn't take Viera long to return. Her face was tight. "The two wizards are tied to chairs. It's apparent they don't want to be here. As for the other eight, my guess is they have some sort of magic too. I don't think they know what they're doing. It looked like they were trying to brew something. One of them was yelling at the two tied up, as if they were expecting answers?"

Betsy wanted to scream and rub her temples at the same time. Both types of magic in one place.

They had so much to deal with and handling it here wouldn't be wise. Instead, she tapped her wrist communicator. "Horax?"

"Pillar Doeth."

"I'm next to a building with ten people in it. Is there any way you can transport them to holding cells, one each. Either on the Ziner, or beneath the government building in New York."

"I can do either. We don't have ten empty rooms but let me check." It took him a few minutes, and Viera looked ready to crack. "Mr. Hopkins said there were ten available cells we could use in New York. He said he expects you to contact him right away. I can send them as soon as the time bubble is dropped."

"Done, Horax!" Viera sounded half-dead.

Betsy closed her eyes and followed the progress of the disappearing people. She wondered if she could put off Juk until their meeting on Monday. As she debated the idea, her phone buzzed in her pocket.

## 20

## *On Boarding*

### Betsy

**B**etsy checked the faces of the people around her. She was pretty sure they were all as tired as she felt. "I'm going to head to New York and sort out these ten people. Viera, I suggest you go—" she faltered. "You're welcome to stay with me. I have guest rooms if you want to stay on Earth, or you can go back to Violet's place. She kept Thorn's room the same."

A yawn stopped her friend from immediately answering. "Gods above, I'm wiped. I'd really like to join you in New York. What time is it ... um, Wisconsin time? Damn this is hard."

"It's just after three in the afternoon." Betsy rubbed her temples. She'd been traveling the world too much lately. "I'm going to contact Violet and ask her to arrange dinner at five-thirty. She could do it for two or three, if you want to join us. Or just go collapse."

Pearl dug in her messenger bag. "I have some of Maleah's brownies. They're good for a couple of hours of pep. Better than coffee, if you ask me."

Betsy barked out a laugh. "Is anything from your town not imbued with magic?"

The girl blushed. "I mean ... no?"

The brownie was small, but it packed a punch. It only took a few seconds for the lightning-like feeling to zap throughout her body, filling her with energy. "Whoa."

Viera laughed. "Can I have a dozen? I could make another time bubble with these."

"Alright, champ," Betsy patted her shoulder. "Let's just go meet Juk. We're both at least mentally fortified to handle him now."

She snorted. "I need popcorn to enjoy the show of you taking him down."

In the end, they all transported to New York. Juk was waiting in the lobby with a tray of coffees and donut holes. When he saw how many arrived, his eyes widened. "Oh, I didn't ... I thought it would just be Betsy and Violet. Where is Violet? Viera? What's going on?"

Marco sighed. "It's fine. I'll go get more drinks. I wouldn't want anyone feeling left out. Then we can head down to the cells in the basement."

The elevator was tucked in a back hallway, far from where anyone would accidentally find it. Juk used a keycard to access it, and it was just big enough for the five of them to fit. They could've probably squeezed in one more person, as long as it was Dulaine or another child.

The small box shot down, and soon they were in a wide, bright corridor. There was a lot of complaining coming from the right, letting Betsy know exactly where the people had been sent.

She got to the first cell and found a scruffy man with long, greasy dark brown hair and gray eyes. "What the hell are we doing here? How did I end up in this cell? I did nothing!"

She stepped up to the bars and spoke in German. "Nothing? You didn't capture two people and tie them to chairs after claiming to be a legit training center?"

His face closed down.

Down the line, a woman groaned. "Please untie me from this chair. I think my arm is broken."

Marco headed down the hall. A moment later Betsy felt the push of magic. He looked over. "She's fine. No broken bones." He faced the cell. "Juk, can you let me in? She needs to be freed."

A moment later Betsy heard a sigh. "Thank you."

"Can you tell me what happened?" Marco sounded calm.

"I thought they were going to teach me how to control this new thing in me ... or take it away. But then they just started to yell at me. Why did they yell at me? I don't know how to do magic. They were supposed to teach me, not the other way around." She sounded both desperate and despondent.

Marco squatted. "Do you want to go to a legitimate school?"

As he spoke with her, Betsy found the other person, another woman, who was tied to a chair. With a small push, she disintegrated the ropes and bindings. She peered at Betsy, terror in her eyes. Then she snapped her head to where Marco and the other woman spoke.

"I don't want to end up like this again," the woman spat. "Or in a cell."

Before Betsy could answer, Marco spoke to the other woman, his voice soft. "You are here because we needed to empty that building, and this was the easiest way to do it. You are free to go. We can send you home. If it's okay, we'd like to give you information about our school. When you're ready, we'd like you to visit the school, meet the other students, learn that where you were wasn't who we are. If you give us a chance, I give you my word, you can go home at any time?"

"Can I have my phone?"

Zuza stepped forward. "We don't know where your phone is, love, but we can give you a phone to contact anyone you want."

The woman in front of Betsy nodded. "Yes. If I can call my family, I agree to your training. I love education and would like to go to the school, but I don't want to be in a cell."

Tension left Betsy's body and she nodded.

Juk nodded. "Okay. You can take the two women. I will arrange what happens with the other eight. I think their consequences are outside your purview, do you agree?"

Viera and Pearl moved to help the two out of the cells, speaking quietly with them.

For once, Betsy agreed with him. "Yes, I'll leave them to you, but remember, we think they have magic. And I'm glad to see you actually remembered the earpiece."

He blushed. "Horax demanded it when we spoke."

Betsy bit the inside of her cheek to stop herself from reacting. "One more thing, do you think we need to meet tomorrow?"

He sighed. "I just need to make sure you all are on top of the influx of people asking for spots in the school."

Marco nodded. "Ania knows. She almost has the Australian school ready. She said she can start getting students Wednesday. We just need more teachers, really."

Pearl smiled. "We may be able to help. I think some Oz residents want to volunteer."

Juk tensed. "Okay, we need to talk tomorrow. This is a lot of information, and I need to make sure it's all recorded."

"Okay, but how about tomorrow afternoon?" Betsy's head swam with exhaustion.

"Fine." His face twisted up, and he pulled out his phone. "Two, local time?"

"I'll be there. I don't know who else, but you'll have me."

Zuza and Marco offered to take the two women to their families to let them know they were alive. Betsy wanted to get to Oz to figure out who the new instructors would be. She headed there with Pearl and Viera.

When they landed in the field outside the one-room schoolhouse, they found Balzeno sitting at the small table, sipping tea with Devlin and Flower Prancer. Despite her shock at seeing the cantankerous Elder, Betsy forced herself to maintain a neutral face as she stepped towards them.

Pearl gaped, "A unicorn," in a breathless voice.

Ignoring her, Betsy smiled neutrally. "Elder Balzeno, Elder Flower Prancer, Devlin." She took a deep breath. "It's lovely to see you all." Betsy turned to the yonat. "Flower Prancer, to what do we owe the honor of your presence here, on Earth, not to mention in Oz? I didn't know you were here. Have you checked in?"

"Pi—Elder Doeth, I just arrived and heard you were on a mission. I checked in with Mr. Hopkins and Pillar Stewart in Australia."

Everything in Betsy felt like she'd been stung with frozen pins and needles. *Did he just call me an Elder?* Next to Flower Prancer, Balzeno snickered.

"What did you call me?" Betsy asked, after she slowly closed her mouth, which had been hanging open.

Flower Prancer's tail swished, indicating his annoyance. "Do not play, Elder Doeth. One does not rise in the ranks without knowing they've been tested. The exercises are clear, and the final words of welcome have always been the same."

After a moment of staring down the yonat, she slowly shifted her gaze to the dwarf. "That's why you tried to burn down my forest. That's why you feel different now, as does the yonat. And those were the weird words you said to me when you left. My elevation is complete? That's it? The full ceremony? Why didn't you just tell me what you were doing?"

Flower Prancer snorted, shaking his head. "What more did you want, Elder Doeth? A full celebration in your name?"

She clenched her jaw to stop herself from rolling her eyes. She was an Elder now ... not only in years. She'd passed the test of mastering three proficiencies. As rare as it was to find in the galaxy, she'd actually entered the rank of Elder. A giddiness bubbled within her.

"It never occurred to me you didn't know the proper ceremony, young Elder," Balzeno said, his words less abrasive than Flower Prancer's. "The lessons taught here are sorely lacking. It is one of the things I told my people. Your school needs better instructors. I intend to teach master classes, and not only to the new students. You and the other Pillars need more direction."

Cold dread filled her, followed by amusement. "You'll be one of our new teachers, will you? In Africa or Australia?"

"Africa. We'll keep Africa purely for the wizards. Australia will be the hybrid with wizards and witches," Balzeno explained.

Both Betsy's brows shot up. "Oh, and who decided this?"

"It's what we've been discussing. Devlin will be one of the magic teachers. He's only needed in his store to create his gems. He has enlisted a few others to teach. This town imbues gems, paper, food, lotions, and liquids. He's found people of each discipline to join him in Australia. It will be good."

Betsy forced herself to smile. "Have you spoken to either Kafi or Ania about this? Or are y'all just making final decisions on your own?"

Flower Prancer's tail flicked again. "I do not see why we would need to consult anyone. We are the Elders here. If you feel we need to ask permission," his voice shifted to a mocking sneer at the last two words, "as the youngest Elder, please, take our plans wherever you feel they need to go."

A laugh burst from her. "Oh, no, pony boy, you do your own errands. I am busy enough around here. Now, if you don't mind," she turned to Devlin, "I'd like to meet these volunteers. I'd also like at least one or two magic teachers in Africa. I don't want it to be quite as split as you all have set it up."

Devlin shot up to his feet. "Are you sure?"

"Yes. I think everyone should be given the opportunity to learn what you do here. Some of it is beyond fantastic."

The smile that took over his face was worth the compliment.

## 21

*Alone In The Woods*

### Dulaine

Her body was stiff, but she'd been moved to a different bed. What she lay in was bigger, softer, and had a canopy.

*Why aren't I in my room? Where are my parents and Pearl?*

Dulaine groaned as she stretched out her body, feeling her muscles complain with the movement. *God, how long have I been in the same position? Am I sick? Should I be worried?*

Her heart started to beat faster, then the memory of the dark room full of boxes came back to her and she forced her eyes open.

The lights were off, but the room was no longer dark, there was light coming in from windows. It had to be a different room if there were windows.

She lay in a four-poster bed with a flimsy, see through, white canopy above her. The bed was pushed against the wall to the left, but there were large windows lining the wall. Dulaine could see the tops of trees, but it was too dark to see details. She thought it was the start or end of a sunny day.

*I hope it's dawn; I'd like to get a better view of where I am.*

She pushed herself up to a sitting position and swung her legs over the side of the bed. She had to extract herself from several thick, warm blankets. On the table next to the bed was a steaming mug. Lifting it, it smelled like an herbal tea. She debated not drinking, but if these people wanted to poison her, it would've happened by now ... and she was thirsty.

With a sigh, she lifted the offering and sipped. The warm drink immediately began to comfort her and her muscles relaxed.

The room she was in was bigger than her bedroom at home. The bed was large—it would fit three or four of her. To the left were sliding doors that looked like they led to a balcony. There were two doors across from her, a dresser, and a small sitting area with a comfy chair and a table.

*I hope one of those doors leads to a bathroom.*

Dulaine put the tea down and tried to open each door. One was locked. The other was a closet with clothes, but through the closet was another opening that led to a bathroom. She quickly used the facilities. The closet was full of items that all looked to be her size. "How long have I been here?" she asked herself softly.

Her stomach clenched with the thought of how long it'd been since she'd been with her family. *Do they miss me?*

Feeling sticky, she found an outfit, a light purple top, and cream pants with a tie top. Then she went to take a shower.

Once clean, she felt more human. The clothes were a bit off. They had extra buckles and ties, but they fit, and that was what she found important.

Back in the main room, there was a plate with pancakes and sausage links on the table by the overstuffed seat. They hadn't been there when she'd entered the closet. She carried the food to the deck, where she found a table and wood chair that would be more comfortable for eating. Then she headed back in for her tea. It wasn't as warm, but it was drinkable.

It was warm outside and dark. She couldn't see much, but it looked like she was in a wooded area on the side of a hill. She couldn't hear the sound of birds, but the enclosed area allowed for a slight breeze.

The pancakes tasted like they were made by someone who'd only ever seen a picture of the meal but had never actually tried them. The sausage was just strange. *I wonder if these are vegetarian sausages.* Her hunger made it all taste better.

Once she finished, she did a more detailed search of the space she was in. The deck was enclosed with a mesh screen, no escape there. The room was sealed, the windows didn't open, no escape there.

As she poked through everything in the room, she couldn't figure out anything that would give away why anyone would want her.

A commotion outside the building got her attention.

She ran to the deck and below, on the ground, she saw a herd of horses running past.

Squinting, she saw they were white, brown, and black beasts. There could've been other colors, but it was too dark for better details. She saw something glinting in the setting sun ... or was that moonlight?

*God, where am I?*

# 22

*Traveling The World*

## Betsy

Monday morning, Betsy and Viera walked the paths through the woods on her property. A sense of calm seemed to come over her friend. "You appear happy."

Viera's head fell back as she gazed up at the clouds dotting the sky above them. The ven zoomed back and forth, playing in the leaves. "I am. It's nice being here, you know, where the animals and the trees all make sense."

"Make sense?"

"Well, nothing is shifting form or size and none of the animals have six legs." Viera chuckled. "Don't get me wrong, I really love it there, and learning about everything on a new world is ... it's exciting, Betsy, but some days I miss easy."

"I understand that." She bumped shoulders with her friend.

"Being here, blending in, understanding everything, it's nice. I do want to get back to Thorn ... *home* to Thorn, but I feel like I'm getting refilled."

"Ms. Kor, check this out!" Up ahead, Scout ran down the path, touching and feeling everything. "I don't think I've ever seen flowers like this. And have you seen Buttercup? She's so much bigger than any of the others. The female ven are always the biggest of the species. She may end up bigger than Beaver."

He kept on talking about everything he saw. Betsy smiled at the boy. "You're going to have fun teaching him."

"I've loved teaching him for the last year, not to mention him teaching me. I don't see it ending any time soon. He's so curious." Viera watched as Scout disappeared around a turn.

"I got a message from Horax that he found magical beings in South Africa. There were other locations in Africa that he picked up, but Kafi said he knew about the areas as religious hot spots. He said he doesn't think they're involved." Betsy enjoyed the breeze that ruffled the leaves.

"Just one country? I may not even want him to narrow it down. Where's the challenge?"

They laughed, then Scout yelled from within her woods, "Ms. Kor! Pillar ... um, Elder Doeth! There's been an attack!"

Viera ran. Betsy sighed but jogged after her. She was pretty sure about what she'd find.

The two stood near a dead tree with a hole through the trunk about a meter and a half above the ground. It was the perfect height for Scout to look through, like a weird spy hole.

Viera's brow knit. "What do you think happened here?"

Betsy grunted. "I happened." She quickly explained Balzeno's visit and the test.

"And he never told you that you were being tested to become an Elder?"

"No. And until Flower Prancer called me out, I had no idea."

Viera curled her lips in and her eyes widened.

Betsy shook her head. "Go ahead and laugh. I get it."

The giggles echoed around the woods, loud enough to disturb birds, squirrels, and other wildlife. "Are any of the Elder's easy? Between Flower Prancer's arrogance and Balzeno's loftiness, they're all just so ... I don't know, insufferable."

The cacophony of noise broke through Betsy's annoyance, and she smiled at her friend's joy.

"So, when do we head to South Africa, and where exactly are we going?"

"We're going to Lesotho. Maseru, Lesotho, to be exact." She smiled at Viera's look of bafflement. "Horax said he'd have more locations later today or tomorrow. He will be looking at North America next."

"Sounds good. To be honest, I've heard of Lesotho, just never Maseru."

Betsy patted Viera on the back. "There's nothing that says you have to have heard of every place, but how do you know of Lesotho?"

Viera's smile grew. "There was a person on staff who had been in the Peace Corps there. He started just about every sentence with, 'When I was in Lesotho...'"

Once Scout had his fill of the tree with a hole in it, they headed back to the house. Scout was sent to Violet and Betsy arranged with Zuza and Marco, who would bring Pearl, to meet in Maseru.

When they got a block from where the compound was, they found guards circling the area. Zuza grumbled under his breath. "How many of these wankers do we need to worry about?"

Viera shut her eyes and clenched her jaw. "A lot. Maybe a dozen. I think they have a couple dozen people in a building in the center. I'm not sure if they're in there by choice or under duress."

Pearl looked around the street. "There are so many people here, but we don't really blend."

"No, we don't," Betsy agreed. "So, we'll walk around, acting like tourists, and try to get close to the building. We need to see if we can figure out how many people are in the building, and if they want to be there."

They only made it about a block before they were surrounded by a group of men and women who didn't look friendly. Zuza gave a small signal as he took point, speaking with one of the men blocking them. "Can I help you?"

"No English."

Zuza smiled and shot a look over his shoulder at Marco. Marco sighed and stepped forward. "What seems to be the problem?"

He spoke in Sotho. Languages were a pet project of his. Betsy wasn't sure how many he spoke, but she stopped being shocked when he pulled another one from his back pocket. She only knew it was Sotho because that was the common language in these parts and all the eyes of the people surrounding them widened after he spoke.

The man who declared 'No English' narrowed his eyes. "What are you doing around here? You don't belong."

Marco bowed his head. "We're just taking in the sights, seeing what your fine city has to offer. Do you have a suggestion of a better place for us to walk? This area seems lovely."

"Anywhere but here. Go. Now."

Betsy closed her eyes. There were six men and women in front of her. One by one, she reached into their minds, starting with the one in the back. *'It's late, you want to go home. Your shift is clearly over. These tourists are nobody and it's such a hassle being mad over nothing.'*

After each suggestion, she opened her eyes and watched as the person she targeted shook his or her head, looked around, then turned and walked off.

When there was only the one left, she leaned forward, and whispered with intent, "Sleep under a tree in the park."

His eyes widened and then his face hardened. "That is my final word." Then he spun on his heel and stormed off. Betsy watched as he crossed the street to a small grassy area. He sat under a tree, lifted his knees, and rested his head on his folded arms. As she watched, his body relaxed and she could feel his sleep.

Marco turned to face her. "You're scary, you know that, right? Did you do that to all of them?"

"No, I sent the rest of them home." She turned to Viera. "Now, lead on."

"Right, mind control. Of course." Viera laughed dryly, then led them two more blocks, passing what Betsy guessed were other guards, but without any trouble.

*They probably figured we made it past the first checkpoint, so we were safe.*

With a jerk of her head, Viera indicated which building was their target. Marco leaned on one hand against the side of the structure.

His face tightened. "Gah, two dozen people. They're all clustered in the back. I ... I can't tell if they're stressed."

"I can set a time bubble, but with the guards, all of you will have to be really diligent." Viera's face scrunched up.

"Go," Betsy said. "Hurry."

The magic flooded the area, and Viera disappeared.

A few minutes later, two guards approached them from a side street. "Hey, you. What are you doing here?"

Marco stepped up. "We're just relaxing. We've been walking around all day. In a minute, we'll head back to our hotel. Can you give us directions?"

"Don't relax here!"

Pearl stepped up. She flicked her fingers, splashing the men with drops of liquid. The men shook their heads, then wandered off.

Marco turned to her. "What did you do?"

"It's something my dad cooked up. It's an 'ignore me' and 'go away' all in one. It doesn't last long, maybe ten minutes, but I thought it may be useful."

"Damn." Betsy huffed out a laugh. "I'm going to be the first to sign up for classes. All of you have some crazy spells."

Viera came out. "It looks like about half the people are fine with their situation, the others are unhappy. I say we pull them all out, talk with them, then bring them back."

Betsy shook her head. "Drop the bubble. Let's just go in and speak with them. I'm tired of being subtle."

They entered and followed Viera. When they ran into a guard, Betsy just put them to sleep. She was tired of playing. If they had another compound later today, they'd need a new tactic.

*Maybe we could bring Xantay.*

The fourteen magic users were surrounded by five guards. Pearl created fire, and Viera made an image of a qynad. Betsy hoped there weren't any sensitive electronics that Pearl's magic just destroyed.

Marco bellowed. "Don't move if you want to survive." Then he turned to the wizards, who were behind a caged off section of wall at the side of the room. "We're here to give you a choice. We've opened a school to teach you magic. You'll have your freedom and not be surrounded by people with guns. Come with us, or stay here, it is up to you."

The people gaped at them. "How will you get us out of here?"

"Don't worry, we have our ways. We understand magic." Marco smirked and Betsy and Zuza rolled their eyes.

In the end, ten of them chose to leave. The other four wanted to return home. Betsy called Violet, who arranged the transport. It was nice leaving directly from the building and not having to face all the guards again.

When the world solidified, Betsy found herself in Violet's kitchen. Viera and Scout were there as well. "This isn't what I expected."

"We have the meeting with Juk soon. I thought you'd like lunch." Violet gave her a shy smile. "I figured the others could handle the new recruits."

"Hmm, food. I may love you."

Violet came over and gave her a kiss. "Good. Just remember that feeling when you're being poisoned by what I feed you."

Viera squealed. "Oh, my God, the two of you? That's fantastic! Does that mean you'll end up on Abritos as well?"

They both laughed, but Violet spoke first. "Actually, I think I want to stay here. Sorry."

"Aww. Oh, well, it was worth a hope, no?"

Before Betsy could answer, her phone beeped. She saw it was Horax, and she tensed. *Is this good or bad news?*

Opening up her email, she saw he had sent two more locations, one in Montana and the other in Florida. "The US. One of these may actually have Dulaine. I don't want to get too excited, but this could be it. We have to tell Juk we can't come in today. We need to check these out."

Violet nodded. "Okay, here. Eat this casserole, get your strength up. You both look like you've been hit by a truck. Maybe bring Balzeno, Flower Prancer, or Xantay with you? They can help."

"True." Betsy sighed. "It would just be very obvious."

Viera shrugged. "Me or Flower Prancer could put Xantay under an invisibility cloak. We could use her power without anyone seeing."

"I just don't want the public relations nightmare if anyone does see. Qynads are already feared by so many."

"Okay, no qynad. But Flower Prancer can keep himself under a cloak," Viera persisted. "And he is an Elder with all his magical abilities."

They continued to eat the casserole, which was good. It felt like it stuck to Betsy's bones, in a good way. "I thought you'd want to get away from him, not spend more time."

"Yeah, but he is good at what he does."

"So are we."

After confirming with Juk that he was okay with moving the meeting to Tuesday, Betsy contacted Zuza and Marco. They had their hands full with the new witches in Africa. Ania was busy getting the school up and running in Australia.

In the end, Pearl, Balzeno, and Flower Prancer joined them in Florida. They dropped into Palm Coast. The compound with the wizards wasn't near anything but a small beach and a bunch of palm trees. It was hot, sticky, and a ton of bugs met them.

When they arrived, everyone was outside, having an outdoor meal by the beach. They approached, and were immediately offered a beer, a burger, and a plate of fruit.

Betsy and her friends sat and spoke with the leaders of the Floridian group. They were wizards trying to help others in the area.

"Why didn't you contact us through the website?"

"What website?" A woman asked as she drank her beer. "We just realized all of us were different. We thought we'd start a club, you know, like all the others around here."

Betsy stared at them. "Do you know about the alien invasion last month?"

"Oh, honey, that was just a hoax. You don't actually believe that, do you? It was so fake. Dragons in the air? Blue beings? I mean, I could've put together a better story."

Her head hurt. "So, you believe in magic, but not in the aliens."

"Well, we all seem to have an ability to do something, dear. The proof is in the pudding, isn't it."

With a wave of her hand, Betsy signaled Flower Prancer to drop his invisibility. He snuffled then said in a derisive tone, "Elder Doeth, I do not believe this is a good idea."

"It's not a bad idea. We're slowly introducing the aliens to the public. Since she's convinced they aren't real, no reason to hide."

"Oh, my goodness, it's Starlite, Rainbow Brite's unicorn! And you talk. Did you slip me drugs?"

Betsy rubbed her face. She wasn't sure how much more she could take. Balzeno walked up. "The question, ma'am, is do you want formal training to learn about your magic? You can come to our training facility and then you won't accidentally burn down your fancy club here." He downed the beer he'd been holding.

"Whoa! Who gave this kid a beer! I'm not getting a ticket or going to jail for someone else's neglect! That's it, all of you, out!"

Looking over the faces of the people, Betsy knew Dulaine wasn't amongst the people at the beach party. Moreover, these people weren't the kidnapping type. They were the stick your head in the sand and ignore everything going on around you in the world type. She spun on her heel and walked away.

Pearl ran to catch up to her. "I'll see if Mom, Dad, or Devlin can talk to them. They have a way with ... um, well, irksome people."

Betsy snorted. "Sounds good to me."

They didn't bother with getting too far from the group before finding a place near Missoula, Montana to transport.

Once they arrived, Viera landed on her butt laughing. "My God, that woman wouldn't stop with the alien conspiracy. Flower Prancer appears in front of her? Nothing. Balzeno? More of nothing. She was just ... there was no convincing her. She was worse than my parents. I should go back and introduce them. They'd be besties in no time!"

Her friend's amusement seeped into Betsy, and she finally smiled. "Okay, let's go. After this, maybe we'll find Dulaine."

Pearl sighed. "I hope so. I want Du-Drop home. I miss her and I bet she's scared."

Balzeno looked around. "This feels a bit like some of the worlds I've visited, almost like mine. Mountains, woods. What do you think, Flower Prancer, does it remind you of home?"

His tail swished. "Are you referring to Qazah? I have never been to that planet, Elder."

"Huh? Really? I would've thought it would be of interest to you. Elder Yonat."

"Why?" Flower Prancer snapped. "It has been almost five times the length of my life since my kind populated that planet. There is no reason to visit." His tone spoke volumes. It was not a place he ever wanted to see.

*I wonder what happened on Qazah. War? Poison? The death of magic?* Betsy couldn't imagine what would've happened to cause the yonat species to relocate and never look back.

His tone got through to Balzeno who merely nodded. "Very well. It's a lovely place to visit."

"Never." He turned. "Elder Doeth, where and when are we going?" he snapped.

There was an underground bunker with an above ground structure out in the woods. It was away from town in the middle of nowhere.

As they approached, the feeling of life below called to Betsy. "I feel several people underneath us, but there's someone above as well. Let's start up there, they may be a guard who can call out for help. Then we can go beneath."

Balzeno touched her arm. "Why don't you and Pearl go up top? The three of us will head below ground. We can nip this spot in the bud and get home."

It took Betsy a moment to think through the logistics, but she nodded. "Okay, sounds good."

Pearl pulled her aside. "Okay, let me splash you with the 'ignore me' liquid."

Once that was done, they walked up a dirt path to a surprisingly modern frontier log home with large windows.

A loud sound behind them made them both jerk, jump, and flip around. A herd of wild horses ran past, their fur shining in the sun, which was mostly blocked by the thick foliage above.

The two looked at each other and silently laughed. Then they made their way to the door. Betsy twisted the handle and was about to disintegrate the metal lock when the door swung open.

The door's movement was as quiet as a breeze and the two entered and slowly closed it behind them. The wide windows let in enough light to navigate to the stairs. The only life sign Betsy felt was upstairs.

As they slowly made their way up, step by step, hunched over and gazing every which way, the steps weren't nearly as quiet as the door. Every squeak caused Betsy to flinch.

Once they got to the top, she was happy the feeling she got led them down the hall and not around the area that overlooked the open living room.

Each door entered into an empty room. The third door on the right was locked. She and Pearl looked each other in the eyes, both getting themselves ready for whatever they found.

With a small push, Betsy turned the lock to dust. She hoped the door would open as silently as the main door. However, as she pushed it wide, the sound of metal whining echoed through the house.

Her heart stopped before pounding hard and fast. She swallowed, trying to calm her nerves.

"Damn it!" a woman grumbled from the other side of the door. "I thought I said to leave me until dinner at seven. Is it that late? Are the kids downstairs complaining? Do you need me to knock some sense into them?" There was an audible yawn after she snapped out her question. "Why are you here, for fuck's sake? Talk to me."

Betsy shut the door and melted the metal together. She didn't trust the woman ... or anyone willing to knock sense into kids. Waving her hand, she signaled Pearl to follow her. They raced down the stairs and out of the house. They headed to where they had separated from the others. When they got to the opening to the underground bunker, she didn't feel anything.

Before Pearl could barrel down the steps, Betsy pulled the girl behind a tree. Tapping her wrist, she contacted Horax. "Report, please."

"I've sent the others to the school. Do you want to join them?"

"Yes, please send us there."

They heard the yelling from the upper deck of the house. "Help! I can't get out of my room. Where are you louts?!" Just as the woods melted away.

Once they got to Africa, Pearl ran to the new people. Betsy watched as her face fell more and more with each person. "No, no, no. She's not here. Where is she? Where is Dulaine?"

## 23

## *I Will Not Tell A Lie*

## Betsy

For the next few days, Horax couldn't find any other compounds. After breaking them up, others didn't seem to be popping up very fast. Juk had worked with the government in the locations they'd been. Local authorities were watching the people and groups who hadn't been arrested who were connected to the unsavory organizations. They were making sure no one else got taken.

Many people in Oz were upset and frustrated that Dulaine hadn't been found. Betsy promised she wasn't done looking. She had to spend part of her downtime in the schools. The number of people who had contacted the website had grown, and she was needed to help teach, at least part time.

She told Juk that Thursday's press conference in LA would be her last.

Since Violet was working with Horax on the final numbers and names of who he'd take back with him, she wouldn't be able to join her in front of the camera. Viera finally decided to visit her family. Betsy decided to go a different route.

To Betsy's left, she couldn't believe how happy Devlin looked to be sitting at a press conference. *Why couldn't Violet be here again? Was organizing her people heading home that important? Gah!*

She shot a glance to her right and saw Balzeno. His smirk and the twinkle in his eye may not have been obvious to some, but she knew the dwarf well.

She shook her head and waited to see what this group would ask them.

Janice Werth, an icon of screen and stage, smiled and waved her hand about. Betsy just couldn't bring herself to listen to another introduction.

Devlin leaned in. "I can't believe we're so close to her ... she's ... oh, my God, even as clueless as we are in Oz, we all know who *she* is."

Betsy slid her eyes to his, her face a mask of pleasant neutrality. "You're on camera, gem boy. Our mics aren't on, but they will be soon. You can meet her afterwards."

"Oh! Yeah, right." His eyes widened a bit. "Wait, really?"

"... the panel." Janice's voice rang out.

"Thank you for having us." Betsy sat up a bit taller. "As Janice mentioned," *I hope*, "I've brought a couple of new friends today. In previous press conferences we've spoken to you about Elders, the group who help govern the vastness of the galaxy. Now that aliens and magic are known to our planet, keeping our borders locked down will be more difficult." A murmur started in the crowd. "Both to aliens who want to come visit a planet denied them so long as well as us ... humans, curious about up there." Betsy pointed up.

"That's an option?" A man in a vintage *Aliens* movie shirt asked, his head snapping to look at the ceiling before dropping back to Betsy. "We could leave Earth and explore?"

She sighed. "Ideally? No. If we're to progress as a people like we should, we'll get there in our own time. And believe it or not, we're not far off. Once we've figured it all out, getting to and meeting other beings would have happened fast. That said, now that things have occurred in the," Betsy rolled her hands around each other, "alternative order, as a planet, I don't see our path to space travel will take long."

She waited while the mass of people sat stunned. Some wrote in notebooks, others spoke into their devices. "Okay," Betsy continued. "As we will be dipping our proverbial toes into space, and, in all likelihood, aliens will want to visit us," she looked pointedly at Balzeno and people in the crowd laughed lightly, "Elder Balzeno, one of the leaders, has offered to come to Earth, to help us with training, adapting to everything that has happened, and keeping unsavory elements out."

A woman in the front row pointed her pen at Devlin. "Are you also an alien?"

Devlin blanched. His head swiveled to Betsy, then back to the woman, then he shook it and smiled. "Um ..." He'd leaned in too close, and the microphone echoed his voice like they were at a concert.

Betsy bent over. "Relax. Just talk to her. You'll be fine."

"Right." He leaned back. "Sorry. No, I'm just a human from a town in the south ... um, Southern US. But we've been using magic for generations." Like a wave, the audience swayed forward. "But not like Pillar ... Doeth or Elder Balzeno." He licked his lips and looked at Betsy with wide eyes. She nodded. She didn't want to change her title at this point; it would just confuse the masses.

As for him discussing Oz, the town had agreed to do this, but years ... centuries of keeping a secret made opening up hard. "I ... well, I use magic versus having magic within me. I can tap into what's around me. You may have seen this distinction on the website. Well, I'll be the main teacher for those of you coming to us with this secondary type of magic."

A girl on the side of the room bit her bottom lip. "How is that different?" Something about her had both Betsy and Elder Balzeno taking note.

"Well," Devlin said, a smile on his face. Teaching was something he seemed to love. "For me, I like to figure out spells, simple, complex, the more complex the better, and put them in gems." He pulled out three aquamarine stones, each the size of a small pebble, which made sense considering the cost of the gem. The light blue glinted in the lights of the room. "For instance, I have a truth detector in these. They'll glow when they detect a lie." He placed one in front of himself, Betsy, and Balzeno. "I really only needed one, but I liked the idea of each of us having our own."

The girl's head tilted to the side, her dark brown hair flopping forward over her glasses. "Do you need to prime them to work?"

"I do. The magic will eventually wear down."

A man in the middle scoffed. "We don't care about your stupid stones." All three glowed and the man hunched in on himself.

The woman in the front narrowed her eyes. "Tell us an easy truth and an easy lie ... all of you."

Devlin nodded. "My name is Devlin. My name is Tom."

As predicted, there was only a glow for Devlin's second statement.

Betsy said, "I'm here to help all of you learn about what's going on with aliens and magic." There was no change from in front of her. "My name is Tom." The stone glowed.

Elder Balzeno smiled. "I am sitting on a chair. I am sitting on the floor."

Betsy gazed over the crowd. "Do you all feel better about the stones?"

There was a general buzz of agreement from the people facing them.

"Okay, are there any questions for me, Devlin, who will be joining the school in Africa, or Elder Balzeno?" Betsy felt a tension in the room. She'd been to many press conferences, but she felt less in control today even than when the qynad joined them. *Is it because Violet isn't here? Does having the other woman here help to relax me?*

"Are you going to be teaching both types of magic?" The question came from a woman near the back.

Devlin nodded. "That is our hope. Though not everyone can do what I can, there is a way to determine if you're a wizard, someone who does magic like Pillar Doeth and Elder Balzeno, or a witch, someone who does magic like me. The website has been updated. You can go there to figure it out or just fill out the form and have someone come and help you figure it out."

The woman continued. "Are there people who can do both types? A wizard and a witch?"

Eyes wide, Devlin turned to Betsy. "We think so. We're digging deeper into the different types of magics. We do know that the magic Devlin used to create the stones in front of us tends to mess with technology while what I use doesn't. We're lucky that the magic used to create the stones was done a long time ago allowing us to utilize the stones and cameras today." She waited for the reaction before continuing. "That said, he can do things that are amazing. He created the gem that allowed Xantay to speak at the last press conference. In most of the galaxy, we either use rooms with translation technology and magic or earpieces that translate. Devlin's solution was slick and brilliant."

He smiled wide at her compliment.

The man with the *Aliens* shirt asked, "Are you the same kind of dwarf as in Lord of The Rings?"

Elder Balzeno laughed. His whole body shook with his mirth. Betsy tensed, worried about his answer. "In a way, yes. When Gandalf inspired the writer, he did use my people, though I doubt I'm in the book myself." He turned to Betsy and cold dread washed through her. "Did your grandfather ever say one way or another if anyone specific was in the book?"

The room grew tense. Betsy saw eyes dart from Elder Balzeno, to her, to the stones, which hadn't changed in brightness.

Before Betsy could answer, Devlin asked with a shaky voice, "Gandalf is real ... and he's your grandfather?"

## 24

*A Shortcut To Language*

### Viera

The hot tub water seeped into her body. Viera sat with Betsy and Violet in Betsy's backyard. The ven slept in a patch of sunlight on the patio.

*I didn't know the beasties could be so still.*

Betsy slid lower in the water. "So, you'll be in the language box from here to Abritos?"

"No. I guess Flower Prancer knows how to start it up and it only needs four to five days to finish my lessons. Putting me in it for the full time isn't needed." She shimmied her shoulders. "I'll be able to hang out with Scout until we get to Torville Station Number Six. Now, get this, I don't know if I shared. Tiffany and her parents are moving to Abritos to be liaisons. If I were to guess, they're dropping their daughter off with me and Thorn and slipping into the water. They got used to being alone and can't handle either other cambpulpo or their daughter full time."

A low grumble came from Betsy. She liked the girl. "That girl is the easiest child to be with, and I'm saying that having spent lots of time with Scout."

A small laugh came from Violet. "I don't know that even Thorn would disagree with you."

Viera sighed. "How much time do I have before I need to be on the ship?"

Violet leaned her head back. "We should head in and get you a last meal. You should also stock up on Vegemite. You'll be all the rage."

Her friend shivered but nodded. "I already have. It's like bringing cigarettes to jail. If you have what everyone wants, you become instantly popular, even if you don't like the stuff."

They got out, and Viera took her last water shower for a bit. Then they ate donuts and ice cream sundaes. It wasn't healthy, but it had to last her for a long time. She took a steak sandwich and a peanut butter and jelly sandwich for the road ... so to speak.

Betsy handed her a green stone.

"What is this?"

"It's a piece of jade. It's what the people of Oz use to communicate." She dug in her pocket and pulled out one of her own ... a tad darker. "You just give it a bit of intent for who you want to speak with. It's like a magical walkie-talkie."

Viera took it, dumbfounded. "I hope I'm never not amazed by magic. This is fantastic. I want to learn all of this type of magic, but I have so much of my own stuff to learn, first. Maybe in a few years you can send a few of the Oz people to Abritos so I can learn all of this cool new stuff." She snorted. "As if it's new."

Her friend chuckled. "Maybe."

The stone was solid, but tiny. "What's the range on this thing?"

"Well, that's the question, isn't it? I promised Devlin we would see if we could play around with that. Why don't you tell me at a few key points? Maybe by the edge of the solar system, near the

GPS? On Torville Station Number Six? I think that's where it'll fail. If not, when you're out of the box on Abritos."

"Okay." Viera nodded. "That works."

Betsy patted her back. "Ready to hit the road?"

The line from *Back to the Future* flashed through her mind. *Where we're going, I don't need roads.* Not that she was traveling through time, but it sort of felt that way.

"I feel bad that we couldn't find Dulaine. I don't like failing."

"You didn't fail ... we didn't fail."

Viera huffed out a laugh. "Maybe if we both say it enough, we'll both believe it."

"Exactly."

She hugged Betsy like she'd never get the chance again and then called the Ziner and transported to her room aboard the ship.

For the two-day trip to Torville Station Number Six, she and Scout played games. She tested out her new knowledge of Galactic Standard. There were gaps in what she knew, but it was getting better.

When they docked, Horax reminded them, "You two only have an hour or so, then I expect you back."

Viera shrugged. "We have to find Tiffany and her family. Knowing them, it'll take more than an hour. And while you were orbiting Earth, did you set up a saltwater room for them?"

The qynad's eyes twinkled. "As a matter of fact, I did. Commander Firoza put it on my list, explaining that she didn't want extra drama for my trip. She knew having you along would be drama enough."

Her jaw dropped and Scout laughed. Making a face at her friend, she turned and headed for the promenade. Tiffany and her parents were supposed to meet them at the café, but knowing that family, anything was possible.

She and Scout got a table, and a thrill went through Viera when she realized she could read the menu. When the same server who always helped them came over and asked Scout if they were ready, Viera placed a hand on her menu. "I'm ready. How about you, kiddo?"

His smile lit up the room. "I sure am."

They both told the server what they wanted, and she sashayed off.

That done, Viera gazed around the room. There weren't a lot of beings around them, and some of them were new. Pointing with her chin, she whispered, "What kind of alien are they? I don't recognize them."

His eyes narrowed. "Oh." Then his face tightened. "The one waving his hands, speaking loudly, he's an edraly. I know he looks like us, but usually they have more purple in their skin. You can recognize him by his pointy ears." He bit his lip. "I wonder if his lighter shade is because he's been away from the sun a long time. He's almost as pale as you are Ms. Kor."

The being looked like an elf, but dark. He would disappear in a shadow. *Would that make him a dark elf? Is that a thing? I should've checked out more fantasy books. I'm living in a world where it's all real. Why haven't I done my damn research?*

The elf-looking man guffawed, then he spoke louder. "No, I'm telling you the truth. This box ... it taught the girl my language. Because my language is the same as that of magic, it takes a long time. Like ten to twelve of the Standard Galactic Torville days."

"You left her in there for that long? Why did you want the girl? Who is this brat? And when will you be caught?" His companion screeched out a laugh.

"It took that long to get her to the planet. She's there now. No harm, no foul. As for when I'll be caught, that's just it, I won't. She's from that locked down planet that just discovered aliens. Did you know they have imbuing magic? It's driving the dwarves crazy." He sipped his drink. "No one is allowed in or out, so how could she be anywhere but on that silly backwards rock? I slipped in and nabbed her. She's young enough to both have power and be malleable enough to control. It'll be simple to bend her to my will."

His companion, a gruff looking phoenix, pecked at his bowl. "I hear ya, Yav'til, but you didn't say why."

"Because, silly, she can *imbue*, or so the idiot dwarf told his people. And as good as any of them, to hear him describe it. He wants to train her himself. If I can get her to trust me, then I can start over with the tuvan. Maybe this time I won't mess up. A bit less brain, a bit more brawn, and I can have rideable mounts who can do magic and won't evolve into the arrogant Elder yonats."

Viera's heart beat faster, unable to believe these two spoke so freely in a public area. She tried to hide her interest in their conversation, but she hung on their every word.

"Hot damn." The phoenix squawked. "You stole a girl from Earth to mess with the original beasts you turned into yonats all those years ago? Didn't you get a death sentence in almost the full galaxy because of that? You really are trying to piss everyone off again."

Yav'til smiled, and it wasn't pretty. "If I succeed, I'll earn enough respect to be allowed back onto my planet. I'll no longer be banished. I'll be a hero."

"Do you really think after this long they remember anything but wanting you dead?"

Lights flashed on the promenade, and the edraly peered up. "Well, you're right that someone remembers me. That's my cue. I'm off. The girl will probably be waking up in the next few days knowing a new language. I have someone watching over her, but I need to start teaching her magic. True power has been lost for centuries. In my hands, this girl will be able to challenge the Elders, the real ones, not the silly yonats I created all those years ago."

As he jogged across the promenade and the phoenix flew for one of the sky corridors, Viera and Scout gazed at each other in shock.

Tiffany and her parents walked up to the table. "Hi, Scout. Hi, Ms. Kor!" Her exuberance brought a smile to Viera's face but couldn't distract her from her whirling thoughts. "I'm so happy to see you both again. Is it time to head to Abritos?"

Body trembling, Viera stared from Tiffany to the girl's parents, and then down at Scout. "I'm so sorry. I have to return to Earth—we have to let Betsy know where Dulaine is."

Thank you for reading!
Magic Rewritten

Please Leave a review for this book so others know how much you enjoyed reading it.

Find more information on my <u>books on my website</u>

Harlowe Frost has been a teacher at both the high school and college level. Her parents instilled a love of reading from a young age. She grew up in the queer community. Her favorite genre growing up was fantasy and science fiction, that is, until she discovered urban fantasy and paranormal romance. What she never found in those books was the diversity in background, gender identity, and sexuality she saw in the people around her. She decided if she couldn't find that in what she read, then she would write it herself. This started her writing paranormal romance with a LGBTQ+ background.